Storm Warning

**Center Point
Large Print**

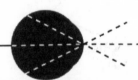

**This Large Print Book carries the
Seal of Approval of N.A.V.H.**

Storm Warning

LINDA HALL

CENTER POINT PUBLISHING
THORNDIKE, MAINE

This Center Point Large Print edition
is published in the year 2010 by arrangement with
Harlequin Books S.A.

The text of this Large Print edition is unabridged.
In other aspects, this book may vary
from the original edition.
Printed in the United States of America
on permanent paper.
Set in 16-point Times New Roman type.

ISBN: 978-1-60285-693-6

Library of Congress Cataloging-in-Publication Data

Hall, Linda, 1950-
  Storm warning / Linda Hall. -- Center Point large print ed.
    p. cm. -- (Whisper Lake series)
  Originally published: New York : Harlequin, 2010.
  ISBN 978-1-60285-693-6 (library binding : alk. paper)
  1. Large type books. I. Title.

PS3558.A3698S76 2010
813'.54--dc22

2009042868

Lord, You have been our dwelling place
throughout all generations.
—*Psalms* 90:1

Storm Warning

ONE

The storm took her by surprise. Somehow, lost in a long and elaborate daydream on this sunny, glorious day, Nori Edwards hadn't seen the sky blackening behind her. She was paddling across the silky water of Whisper Lake, oblivious. It should have been a clue when a sudden gust of wind whipped her hair across her cheek. It wasn't. She merely sighed, stopped, braced the paddle on the top of her kayak, and wound her hair more securely back into its ponytail, and kept crossing the bay from Twin Peaks Island.

The distant rumbling of thunder concerned her only slightly. In the two weeks she'd lived here, she'd experienced only one brief five-minute thundershower. The thunder was nothing to worry about, she thought. She'd be home and dry in the lodge at Trail's End before any serious rain fell. If it even fell at all. She was strong and her arms easily fell into the rhythm of her strokes.

She had taken a little time off from the backbreaking work of cleaning, clearing brush, sweeping out cabins and unpacking in her lodge, for a relaxing paddle out on the lake. She'd gotten in the habit of doing this, heading out on the lake for an hour or two each afternoon.

When she'd bought this property, known as Trail's End, she'd been assured by the real estate agent that people from Whisper Lake Crossing would be lining up to work for her on the cleanup and repairs.

What he hadn't told her was that every worker, every contractor, every builder, tradesman and handyman from Bangor to Portland was working on the northern Maine highway infrastructure.

Maybe she was going to have to take her search further afield and put an ad in the *Shawnigan Sentinel.* The town of Shawnigan was nine miles farther down the lake and much bigger than Whisper Lake Crossing.

On the first day she'd walked through the place, she had fallen under its spell. She'd stood on the wide wooden porch and taken in the deep, green smell of the pines, the gently lapping lake. The sun shimmered on it and turned it almost golden. But it was when the agent took her up to the loft that there was no turning back. Log lined, with wide, high, sunlit walls, a massive brick fireplace and cathedral ceilings, it offered a stunning view of Whisper Lake. It would be the perfect orientation for her art studio.

She had stood at the windows and looked out on the lake and thought, *I want this place. I have a good feeling about this place. This place can finally be a home for me and my family.*

She would buy it. She and her daughters would live in the lodge. They would rent out the cabins. This would be a good place to start a new business, a good place to start over, a good place to paint again.

But that dream would never be realized unless she got some help.

It was getting cooler. She rested from her paddling and zipped her nylon windbreaker to her neck. It was the beginning of June and it was still chilly enough for a sweatshirt underneath. It wasn't the howling wind, two-foot waves and claps of thunder that finally caught her attention—it was the sudden, curious quiet. She stopped, felt a ripple of unease.

The sky to her right was blackening. The distant droning of motorboats was gone. The trees had stilled. Even the birds had stopped their chirping. This sunny, pleasant afternoon on the lake had gone slate-gray and silent. She looked around her. She was farther from home than she realized, farther than she wanted to be. Kayaks should hug the shoreline, not go right out in the middle of the lake. Yet here she was, between the island and the shore.

She located her dock on the hazy horizon and started pushing toward it. She smelled the rain before she actually felt it. Heavy, humid, brassy, it caught in her nostrils. She choked, felt exposed out here, a tiny low-slung boat on a massive body of water.

Thick dollops of water fell here and there. And then the wind started. At first it merely ruffled the lake around her. Gradually, it increased into a snarl.

And then all at once it was bearing down on her and she found herself paddling directly into it. She seemed to be getting nowhere. She zagged a little to the right. Maybe she would have a better chance at the wind if she didn't face it square on.

It's not like she hadn't been warned about the lake. That was a constant theme around Whisper Lake Crossing.

"Whisper Lake," said a woman named Alma whom she'd met at Marlene's Café. "You bought them cottages out there? Them Trail's End cabins? Well, all I can say is mind the lake. She got a mind of her own, she does." And then the woman had gone off shaking her head and muttering, "Bad place, bad place."

Pete and Peach were next. Those two old men seemed to be everywhere; holding court at Marlene's Café, the Chinese restaurant, the post office, Earl's Gas and Convenience.

"So you're the one," Pete had said as he pointed at her about a week ago at the post office.

"The one what?" she'd responded.

"The one who finally bought the place out there. None of us thought anyone would." He spit on the ground before he looked up at some place directly over her right shoulder and said, "Be careful of the lake, then."

The wind whorled around her now, strong and

fierce. Rain slashed at her cheeks. No doubt now, she was getting wet, and not just from overhead. Frothy white waves churned over her boat.

She paddled more furiously, wondering if she was making any headway at all, wondering if her new little lake kayak could withstand a thunderstorm of this magnitude.

God, please help me, she breathed.

All around her was sound—crashing rain, slashing lightning, growling thunder, howling wind. The lake was foamy white and no longer snarled; it yelped and snapped at her like a pack of wolves. She opened her mouth in her exertion and tasted cold rain on her tongue. It became harder to breathe.

Her muscles burned as she pulled, pushed, pulled, pushed through the waves. One huge wave rolled right over her small kayak from bow to stern. Would she tip over? What would she do if she lost her paddle? Her bare fingers were cold and cramped and hurting. If only she had worn gloves. She was wearing her personal flotation device, but what help would that be in this cold, cold lake? Plus, nobody would miss her for days. Her daughters were far away at a Christian camp for the summer. And no one else would miss her. She had no one else. Hot tears mingled with icy rain.

The trees along the shore were thrashing crazily, as if the very ground they were standing on had been shaken by a giant hand. Lightning seemed to strike not more than a couple feet away from her on the water. The fine hairs on the back of her neck stood on end, and not for the first time she felt her skin prickle.

She began to pray. She hadn't prayed in a long time and so this surprised her.

The lake was the color of bronze and sky turned into the kind of deep blue-black that nightmares are made of. She could barely make out the shore and ended up paddling off course for a little while before lightning lit up the sky enough for her to see her dock. Just up ahead. Beyond that, her lodge. And home. And warmth. And safety.

Dear God, she prayed, *please help me. Don't let me be hit by lightning. I need to be there for my daughters. It was bad enough to lose their father. They can't lose me, too.*

There was her dock. She was making progress. Just a little bit, but she was going to make it. A little more paddling. A few more strokes. Keep going. She could see her big wraparound porch and she remembered that she had left all her windows open on this day that had started out so sun filled, so fine. She counted strokes to keep her mind occupied.

Ahead of her and a little to the right it looked like a whirlpool was forming. Could this be possible? She skirted around the eddy as best she could and thought about waterspouts. She knew those tornadoes made of water could be deadly.

Another flash of lightning lit up something else. Or someone. A *person?* Standing astride at the end of her dock covered in a green hooded raincoat and wearing black boots. It was a person, a man, and he was waving toward her.

His hands were cupped around his mouth and he was yelling something that was immediately swallowed up by the storm. She paddled toward him, new hope surging through her.

When she was close enough she saw that he was a big man. A mountain of a man. Water streamed off the brim of his hat like a waterfall. She couldn't see his face.

Miraculously, she surfed on a big wave and foundered only feet from the dock.

"Here!" he called on the wind. "Reach your paddle toward me!"

She did so. He lunged at it with rain-soaked hands. He missed and she thought he would fall into the water beside her.

She prayed her dock would hold. It was one of the things most in need of repair. Constructed of old gray boards with many missing slats, it was somehow anchored to the bottom of the lake with only two stanchions remaining at the end.

She called. "I'll try to get closer."

"Don't let go your end!" he said.

"I won't," she yelled, but not much strength remained in her arms.

She tried again. This time he grabbed it, held on hard and pulled the kayak toward the dock with brute force. When she was abeam the dock, another problem presented itself. "I don't know if I can get out," she yelled up at him. "The wind is blowing me into the boards."

As best she could she reached forward and pulled the rubber apron that encircled her waist and unfastened it from the rim of the cockpit. The entire bottom of the kayak sloshed with water. She was totally soaked through.

He said, "I'll grab hold of you. I'll hold you. I won't let you go."

The next time the kayak pitched toward the dock he reached out and grabbed onto her PFD and held fast. She hoped nothing would rip. He bent down, reached under her arms and brought her up onto the dock beside him. She held on to him while he grabbed the kayak's line and shoved the boat hard up toward the shore. He took the paddle and threw it up onto the beach, as well. He was amazingly strong.

"Let's get out of the rain," he yelled over the wind.

She merely nodded.

"Careful now, careful there," he said, taking her arm. "The dock is slippery. It's not all that sturdy. Hold on to me. There. I've got you."

His voice was gentle for so large a man. And when her feet wouldn't work, when she shivered so much that she slipped on the slick, wet dock, he lifted her up into his arms and carried her. He didn't put her down until they were up on her porch. "Let's get you in and dried off. You're freezing."

She was, but she was also strangely warmed by his closeness.

Before they went inside, she looked up into the face of her rescuer and mouthed, *Thank you.*

Who was this man who had appeared out of nowhere?

The sound of the storm had changed. The lightning and thunder had moved on a bit, but the rain was coming straight down and steady, and so heavy she could barely see the lake.

She was still wearing her PFD and the weight of it added to her cold. She took it off and hung it on a hook just outside her door.

She slipped off her sneakers at the same time and left them there, too. She padded off to the kitchen in wet, bare feet, leaving tracks on the hardwood.

"You can leave your wet things here. Follow me into the kitchen. I'll get you a towel."

Her teeth actually chattered as she retrieved a large towel from a hall closet and handed it to the man who had saved her from the storm. "Here," she said. He took off his wide-brimmed oilskin hat and ran the towel over his head. His hair was pale in color and fell well below his ears. Without his hat he looked younger. She guessed him close to her own age of thirty-eight, or not much older.

She was suddenly conscious of her own drenched clothes. "I'll just be a minute," she said to him. "Make yourself at home."

She closed her bedroom door behind her. *Make yourself at home?* Who was this man she had just encouraged to make himself at home in her house? In her room she quickly shed her wet clothes and donned jeans and a big, comfy sweatshirt. She ran a towel over her hair and pulled it back into a ponytail. Her daughters were encouraging her to grow it. It wasn't quite long enough for a full ponytail, but she kept trying.

When she emerged, he was kneeling in front of the hearth laying in wood for a fire. He had taken off his oilskin jacket and underneath he wore a gray long-sleeved cotton T-shirt and khaki trousers. He had pushed up the sleeves of his shirt and she could see his forearms were all muscle. No wonder he'd had no trouble lifting her out of the water like he did.

Pieces of his hair fell forward over his eyes when he smiled up at her. His eyes were deep and very blue. He said, "I wondered if you'd mind if I made a fire. Warm the place up a bit."

"Mind? That's wonderful," she said. Somehow it seemed perfectly natural that this stranger should be making a fire in her fireplace. She stood there for a moment while he silently lit a match to the newspaper and kindling. When he rose she said, "Now, is there something I can help you with? You drove out here because . . . ?"

"Pretty lucky that I was out here. You were sort of struggling a bit. I'm glad I could come along and help. I was all set to get my canoe down if need be."

She looked out of the window. Another truck was parked right next to her own truck. On his, a long green canoe was upside down over the cab. The two trucks, side by side, looked like a matched set. A dog's head peered out of the truck window.

"You have a dog," Nori said.

A slow smile began on his face. "His name is Chester."

"He looks like he's jumping all over your truck."

"That's Chester."

She looked up at him. Here they were, talking about dogs, and she didn't even know who he was or why he was in her living room.

"Your name is?"

"Oh, sorry." He moved toward her. "I'm Steve Baylor. And you're Nori."

"You know who I am?"

She redid her ponytail more securely in the elastic.

"The rumor around town is that you're looking for a handyman. I've come to apply for the job.

That is, if you haven't already got someone else lined up."

"Well," she said, and moved an errant wisp of hair out of her face. "I am looking for someone."

"I'm your man, then." He opened his arms wide and grinned deeply. He had a very expressive mouth that went up more on the right side than the left when he smiled.

"And you drove all the way out here in the middle of a storm because you want to work here?"

His expression became serious. "I was going to call you. Marlene from the café told me about the job. I was just canoeing the Kettle Stream and saw someone out on the lake and I thought I better go see. I was hoping it wasn't you. You want to avoid thunderstorms on the lake if you can at all help it."

She nodded. "I've been told that before."

He said, "This lake can blow up into a frenzy and then be completely calm in the space of twenty minutes."

She looked out at the lake. The downpour was unrelenting, but the lake looked remarkably calmer.

"So then, Steve, what are your qualifications?" She tried to keep her tone businesslike, yet the memory of being held in his gentle arms was still fresh in her mind.

"I'm strong," he said immediately. "I'm a carpenter and cabinetmaker. I'm a good organizer. I can put in a good day's work."

Nori clasped her hands in front of her. Someone like him was who she needed. "Would you like a hot drink? Something to warm you up? I could make coffee. We can talk more then."

"Coffee would be great."

"Follow me," she offered. "Don't mind the mess. I've been here two weeks and I've been concentrating more on clearing a path to the beach and unearthing places to park."

"That's the sort of thing I could help with."

"I think I need a whole crew."

"My thoughts exactly. I know a bunch of young people—from the church actually—who I could round up."

As they entered the kitchen she tried to see the place through his eyes—boxes leaning against walls, coffee mugs and plates stacked and balanced precariously on counters, piles of papers and books next to the coffeemaker, dirty dishes in sink, her laptop and more papers on the small table. She wanted all new cupboards and countertops. And a new sink while she was at it, and a dishwasher. Actually, she wanted an entirely new kitchen. She was reluctant, therefore, to unpack a lot into cupboards that eventually would be torn down.

The fire was already warming up the place and it felt good. She got a tin of coffee from her pantry, measured fresh grounds into her coffeepot, poured water into the reservoir and switched it on.

He said nothing while she did this, and she didn't know whether she should be talking or not. He seemed to be a quiet man, a nice man, but the silence was beginning to make her uncomfortable. She began talking, her back still to him. "I want to start with this kitchen. Since I plan to live here, this is where I want to begin—"

"For the summer?"

She turned around to face him. "Excuse me?"

"You plan to live here for the summer?"

"Year-round," she said.

"Year-round?"

"Yes, year-round. This lodge is fully winterized. Maybe not the cabins, but the lodge, certainly. The real estate agent told me the road is plowed regularly. And the place is quiet. That's what I'm looking for. A quiet place to live *year-round*." A place to call home, she wanted to add.

Steve said, "He told you they plow the road?"

"Yes. He did."

"Well, I don't know where he gets his information. . . ."

"I'll hire someone then," she said quickly, turning away, her face becoming hot.

A few moments later he said, "Pretty isolated out here."

"I'll manage."

"I'm sure you will. You strike me as a strong woman."

Thankfully her back was still to him. She

didn't know what her face would reveal with that comment.

As she got a couple of mugs from the counter, she heard a loud crash behind her. She jumped and turned, put a hand to her mouth.

"The chair," he said rather sheepishly. "I'm sorry."

Steve was on his backside on the floor, his left leg caught in a broken chair leg, his right stuck out in front of him. He had sat on a wooden rocking chair and gone right through it. It was a chair that had been here when she moved in.

She put a hand to her mouth and started to giggle. She couldn't help it. He managed to disentangle himself and hoist himself up. He was laughing, too.

She said, "I'm sorry. I shouldn't laugh. Are you okay?"

"Only my dignity is tarnished," he said, rising. "And this chair. Sometimes I don't know my own strength."

"I should've told you that chair might be questionable," she said. "I brought it in here because I was trying to figure out what to do with it. You didn't break anything that wasn't broken before."

He picked up the broken front leg and ran his hands over it quietly for a while. Finally, he said, "Can I take the pieces of this chair with me? I might be able to do something with it."

"Be my guest. I wasn't sure it was worth fixing. It's kind of plain."

"This chair? This is a great old chair. It looks like an antique Shaker rocking chair. Their chairs were plain because their lifestyle was plain. I'd love the chance to be able to work on it."

"You sure know your chairs," Nori said, pouring coffee into two mugs.

"I love carpentry."

They sat down at the table across from each other and she spread out her lists and Internet printouts on the table in front of her.

"I've looked at some new cupboards online and found out that a company can deliver them from Bangor. I'll just need someone to bring them out here and install them. Can you do that?" From her stack of papers and home repair and decorating books, she unearthed pictures she had printed from the Web of the kitchen cupboards she was looking at.

He picked up her printed sheet and looked at it for several minutes, frowning before he put it back down on the table. "You don't want those things. They're factory mass-produced. Not for this grand old place. I'm a cabinetmaker. I could make you cupboards. Nice ones. From scratch."

"Great. Okay, well." She felt a jittery jangle of nerves. She knew the price of handcrafted cupboards. Her budget only had so much in it. "But we'll need to talk price." She added quickly, "I also have to order new appliances—dishwasher, fridge, stove, one with two ovens and a separate warming oven. And I've got my budget down to the penny."

"What's wrong with that stove?" Steve pointed at the stove up against the wall.

She stared at him. "That's a *wood* stove."

"Yeah? So? It's a classic."

"I know it's a classic. And it'll stay there. I just don't think I'll be using it to actually cook things."

"No," he said. "You gotta use it. It'll really warm up the place, too."

"Well, even if I use that as a stove, I still want a new, proper, energy-efficient oven. And dishwasher. This washing dishes by hand is for the birds."

Before she had even finished talking Steve was up and examining the cupboard next to the sink. It was empty inside. He closed it, opened it again. She watched in silence while he ran his fingers over the wood as if reading Braille.

He turned. "I can fix you up with brand-new cupboards. We can look at woods. I would recommend something dark. I think that would fit in with the decor of the rest of this old kitchen."

He went on. "If you're going to run a guest-house and retreat center you'll want the best. Nothing prefab for here."

She furrowed her brow and looked at him. "How did you know I plan to open a retreat center?"

"A little birdie told me." And then he chuckled deeply. "Actually, Marlene may have mentioned that."

"Oh. Right." Marlene at Marlene's Café was one of the few people she'd gotten to know. Nori didn't have Internet access at Trail's End yet, so took advantage of the free Wi-Fi at Marlene's Café at least once a day.

While Steve and Nori drank their coffee, she went over the rest of her list and pictures. Next was a tour of the lodge. Steve had a lot of good ideas. When she asked him how he had learned so much about interior design he told her it was the influence of his parents. "My dad did the carpentry work and my mother did the designing."

"So, you worked with your father?"

He didn't answer her question and the tiniest of frowns settled between his eyes.

After they'd gone through every room in the lodge, they decided to take a look at the cabins since the rain had lessened.

The sun began to glisten through wet tree branches as the two of them headed outside.

"Why don't you get your dog?" she said.

After Steve let Chester out of his truck, Nori commented on what a remarkably well-trained pooch Chester was.

"He's had a bit of police training."

"Wow. That must be interesting."

"It is," he added.

Beyond them the lake lapped gently against the shore. It was hard to believe that an hour before it had been a maelstrom.

About an hour later, she and Steve and Chester ended up back in the kitchen going over numbers and ideas. At the end of another pot of coffee and some cookies she had bought at the bakery in town, they came up with a workable plan. Steve would head into Shawnigan tomorrow and look at woods for her cupboards. He had promised her that he could do it for her budgeted amount. Then he would organize work crews. "You'll like the kids from the church," he said.

"I've met Selena, Marlene's daughter. Does she go to church? She's the only young person I know. She seems a bit quiet, though," Nori said.

"All the kids around here are a bit quiet," he said.

She thought that was an odd statement, but didn't pursue it. Instead, she asked, "Are you from around here, Steve? You don't have the accent."

"I'm a transplant. Been here three years."

"Where did you come from?"

"Boston."

They both noticed the smoke at the same time, but Steve got to the fireplace first.

"Sometimes that fireplace smokes." Nori was close behind him. She knelt down beside him and watched him work on the flue.

"Do you think the chimney works properly?"

He fiddled with the knob. "It's the flue. It wasn't opened all the way. It was a bit stuck. I think I got it. But I would get it cleaned. That's part of the problem."

"I'll do that."

"I could give you names."

"Please."

Their faces were at the same level and he was so close she could catch the scent of him. He smelled like the out-of-doors—canoeing and camping.

He said, "Who split all this wood?"

"I did."

He looked at her and raised one eyebrow. "I'm impressed."

"I'm used to hard work." Nori looked away from him. The truth was, she wasn't. Splitting a few logs had taken her hours and she had the blisters to prove it.

The fire was burning nicely now. He said, "I'm glad someone's taken over this place," he said. "It's too good a place to let go."

There was something so tender in his gaze that she found herself backing away lest she be drawn too closely into those deep eyes. Standing, they were face-to-face with her framed photos on the mantel. There were pictures of her daughters, several of her late husband, Marty, one with the girls draped on either side of him, smiles all over everyone's faces.

"My daughters," Nori said by way of explanation. "They're twins. Sixteen. They're working in a church camp this summer. That's their father . . ."

He looked at the picture for a while without saying anything. "I have an eight-year-old son myself. Jeffrey. He lives with his mother down South."

"I'm sorry," Nori said, finding her voice again.

He looked back at the pictures of Daphne and Rachel. "Your daughters are very pretty. You said they're at a church camp?"

She laughed a bit at that. "Yes, a church camp. I haven't been to church in a while, but my daughters never lost the faith their mother did."

Nori hadn't been to church since her husband's funeral. Sometimes she wondered if God had forgotten all about her. He had looked the other way when that drunk had barreled into her young, strong husband, out for an early morning jog. It felt to her that God's back had been turned on her ever since.

"I'm sorry that you lost your faith." His words sounded genuine. He paused before he said, "I just found mine. I'm still finding mine. I still have a lot to work out. Not in God's love to me, but in my own life."

It was an odd sort of moment. She'd had the idea that Steve might be someone she could talk to, that he was a listening sort of man, that he would somehow understand everything she had gone through and why it was that she had lost her faith. But then he had stiffened and his face darkened.

They said goodbye and she stood on her porch and watched until his truck was out of sight.

As she made her way back inside something felt curious. She was sure she'd left all the windows open when she went kayaking. Had Steve shut them all? When would he have had time to do that?

TWO

Nori Edwards was nothing like he expected. Steve leaned against the gas pump at Earl's Gas and Convenience and filled his truck. From Marlene and her husband, Roy, he'd heard a lot about the woman who had bought Trail's End, but he hadn't met her until today. Everyone in town had a comment or two about "that woman who bought Trail's End."

The place had a history, he knew. Five years ago Earl had bought Trail's End from the couple who had run it for fifteen years. They were tired of the upkeep. Earl wanted to winterize the cabins and turn it into a winter rental place.

Shortly after he bought it, Earl fell off a cabin he was roofing and broke a leg and injured his back. It had turned into something that was chronic. He put Trail's End up for sale shortly after he realized his back wouldn't get better.

Yes, the place had a history.

There was nothing wrong with Trail's End. The workmanship in the lodge was exquisite. The location was superb. The view was magnificent. Trail's End had a lot going for it.

It was something else.

It was all about what had gone on out there two years ago. Steve frowned as he hung the gas nozzle back up and went inside to pay.

He plunked his credit card down on the counter. "Chase around?"

Joe, who'd been out of high school for two years, was a year older than his brother Chase. The sons mostly ran the place, now that their father, Earl, was laid up. Chase worked here part-time, but did a lot of other jobs in town.

Joe leaned his long body into the counter and cracked his gum. "Haven't seen him. Why?"

"I may have some work."

Joe picked up the credit card and regarded him with his small eyes. "What kind of work?"

"What I have is general work—heavy lifting, clearing brush, groundwork, digging, drywall, lots of hammering and nailing. If you see Chase let him know I'm looking for him, will ya?"

"I think he went out shooting." He rubbed the side of his thin nose with the end of a pencil. He was staring at Steve.

Steve shook his head. He was not pleased that Joe and Chase kept guns. Steve used to own guns. He didn't anymore.

Joe said, "That work you're talking about, that's up at them cottages, right? Them ghost cottages."

Ghost cottages. Steve put his credit card back into his wallet and said, "They aren't ghost cottages."

He wished Joe and Chase would get back into the church—all the kids for that matter. Many of them had this idea that Trail's End was cursed, inhabited by ghosts, and that serial killers roamed the forest behind the lodge and cabins. There was nothing that he or the pastor in their church could do to shake that. And it all went back to two years ago when a girl, one of their group, had disappeared from that very place. Or so it was thought.

"How was it out there? What's that lady like in real life?" Joe asked.

Steve tried for a deadpan. "Yes, Joe, I'm here to report that I was out there. She was howling at the moon. Already all the cottages are burning, and sacrifices are being offered."

At this, Joe's reptilian eyes went as wide as Steve had ever seen them. He rubbed at a spot beside his nose. "You kidding me, right?"

"No, I'm not kidding. It really happened. Of course I'm kidding."

Steve signed the credit card slip, slapped the countertop with his hand and said, "Just let Chase know I'm looking for him, will ya?"

Back in his truck, Steve tore open some candy and withdrew a few pieces of licorice. "Hey, Chester, whaddya think? You think everyone around here is nuts?"

His dog, who'd been sitting on the front seat, wagged his tail and came over for an ear scratch.

"Back," Steve ordered.

Chester immediately obeyed and jumped into the backseat.

Steve had a couple more stops to make before

home, where he and Chester would go for a long run along the lake. On the way out to find Connolly, another recent high school graduate who had worked for Steve in the past, he thought about the cottages. He knew they weren't haunted, but he also knew that "something" had happened out there, something that so terrified the kids in the town that many of them wanted nothing to do with Trail's End. The mere mention of Trail's End around Selena or Chase made them clam up and turn away. And Nori had bought the place with no knowledge of any of this, as far as he could tell.

He thought about her. He had noticed her wedding ring right away Where was her husband? Her eyes had seemed so sad when she talked about her daughters and their "father."

She hadn't said "my husband," she had said, "their father." Obviously, she and her husband were estranged. Maybe this was a trial separation. Perhaps they were trying to work things out. And then another thought—maybe her husband was, even now, in Iraq or Afghanistan. He knew from experience that some military wives didn't like to talk about deployments. Maybe this accounted for the sadness in her eyes.

God, he prayed. *Help me to be her friend.*

And then there was the matter of her faith. Her daughters went to church. She didn't. She had lost her faith, she said. Did that have to do with the estrangement?

For someone to have found the faith and then deliberately move away from it was something Steve couldn't understand. When he found God it was like a whole new place opened up in his life, a place he had walled off and protected for so many years. Years lived emotionally distant from his wife and son.

But by the time he found God, it was too late. His wife had left him and taken their son and gone to Florida.

He used to blame his former job for wrecking his marriage. Steve had been a part of an elite corps of the military. It wasn't until finding his way to faith in God that he realized it was him, and not his job.

He remembered pleading with his ex-wife, Julie, not to leave and take their son to Florida with her. "How can you leave? How can you take Jeffrey so far from me?" he had demanded, crying. It was the first time he had actually wept real tears in a decade. He had seen so much in the military. He had walled off so much of his life. It was like all of his emotions up to that point had been cauterized.

Julie had flipped her blond hair behind her ears and retorted, "And that matters to you all of a sudden? You're never here anyway. You haven't been here for any of Jeffrey's moments. Not Jeffrey's soccer games, not Jeffrey's school plays, not the first time Jeffrey rode a two-wheeler, not

Jeffrey's music recitals—do you even know what instrument Jeffrey plays? You've been too busy out saving the world from terrorists."

After Julie had announced that she was also in love with somebody else, Steve had taken the ferry across to Vinalhaven, Maine. Halfway across, he'd removed his wedding ring from his finger and thrown it as far as he could into the choppy ocean. That was three years ago.

He still felt he would never be the kind of man any woman could love. He had so much to learn, so far to go.

It was quite ironic. Two months after Julie left, he did just what she wanted. He separated from the military, escaped to Whisper Lake Crossing and went back to the quiet pursuit of cabinet-making. He loved it. Whenever Alec, the local sheriff who also happened to be his friend, would offer him full-time police work he always had the same response; "Full time? Not interested." Occasionally, Steve helped with something that really caught his fancy—like the disappearance of the girl from church and her boyfriend.

That was the last time Steve had been out to Trail's End. They had been out there looking for any sign of two teenagers. They had to satisfy their curiosity by just walking the grounds. Earl refused to let them search the place, and because the evidence was so flimsy, Alec had never been able to get a search warrant.

He quickly found the small house where Connolly lived with his parents and four siblings. When he told Connolly's mother the nature of the work, she pushed her glasses up on her nose, shook her head and said, "No. I don't think he'll want to work out there."

"Come on, Rita, tell him about the job at least. I took the job out there and she needs help."

"I'll tell him. That's all I can promise. If he doesn't want to go, I won't be forcing him. You know those kids are still traumatized."

Steve got back into his truck and drove down the driveway to Flower Cottage, where his friend Bette and her son Ralph lived. The white house with the flower baskets under each window came into view. As always, the place looked pristine. It reminded Steve of a quaint little English country cottage. Not that he would know what a quaint little English country cottage looked like.

Bette and her forty-year-old son, Ralph, had emigrated from England forty years ago and Bette had brought with her her English accent and her country garden ways. Ralph was a bit slow and simple, yet capable of a good day's work. Rumor had it that when Ralph was about five, Bette's husband went back to England. He just couldn't take the responsibility of a mentally disabled son. No one had heard from him since and Bette never talked about him.

Steve parked his truck next to Bette's Volvo

and as he and Chester got out, Boris, their springer spaniel, ran over, tail wagging and tongue flapping. Steve had a certain affection for the old dog. Despite the male name, Boris was Chester's mother. The two dogs took off down the expanse of lawn that Bette still referred to as a "garden" even though she'd been in Maine for years.

Bette and Ralph were out back piling dry weeds into a wheelbarrow. Bette waved when she saw Steve, and came toward him, pulling off garden gloves.

"Hello, Steven. How lovely that you're here."

He smiled and said hello. It was like this little place on the planet was infused with peace. Coming here was like coming home. Bette had become almost a mother to him.

"Are you staying for supper?" she asked. "I've got a chicken in the Slow-Cooker."

"Didn't come for that express purpose, but I'll never refuse an offer of a meal here. I came about work."

By this time, Ralph had appeared, wearing a grass-stained pair of khakis and a baseball cap.

"Hey, buddy," Steve said. "How's it going?"

"Good. Good. Good. Working hard. Working here. Lots to do."

"You want to work with me for a while?"

Bette's eyes lit up. "Really, Steve? You have a job for Ralph?"

Steve nodded and grinned, and then to Ralph

he said, "But it's hard work. You up for a bit of hard work?"

"Yes, Steve. I can do hard work. I can."

Ralph was a big man with a big heart. Steve had used him before on work projects.

"The work is up at Trail's End, for someone named Nori Edwards."

Ralph dropped the handles of the wheelbarrow, and it clanked down onto the flagstones. He frowned and shook his head. "No. No. Can't go there. Not there. No. Not over there. Mum. No."

"Ralph," Bette said. "It's okay. Nothing out there can hurt you."

But the young man was shaking his head over and over. "Can't go there. Can't go there. Can't go . . ." He kept repeating it over and over.

Bette put her arm around her son. "You've been listening to Earl's boys. They put all sorts of silly things into your head. There is nothing to be afraid of there."

Yet Ralph's eyes were wide. "But there is . . . there is . . ."

Bette, her arm still around her big son, smiled up at Steve. "He'll come. We'll talk about it over tea."

Lately, Nori always had the feeling that she was forgetting something. She would walk out of a store and when she got to the door she would make a point of turning and looking back to make sure she hadn't left anything on the counter. Or when she got out of her car she would mentally count the items she was carrying—bag over shoulder, sunglasses on head, keys in hand, cell phone in pocket. Even when she counted, even when she looked back, she still felt as though she was leaving something important behind.

It didn't used to be like this. Marty always told her that she was the most organized person he knew. She had to be. When you were married to the most head-in-the-clouds individual on the planet, one had to compensate. Marty, her sensitive, artist husband, could be so into a painting that he would lose track of everything—time, appointments, meals. She was the one in the family who made sure the girls got to piano lessons and gymnastics on time. She was the one who would make sure they had regular family meal times and that Marty was called in, precisely at six, from whatever piece of art he was working on. She made him see the importance of that.

When Nori complained that she had to do all the thinking around the place, all the organizing, all the setting down of schedules, Marty would take her in his arms and call her his primary color, the color from which all other colors got their hues; that without her, there was no color at all.

The color thing wasn't entirely true. If she had been the primary color, then Marty had been the palette where the colors were mixed and made usable, because when he'd died her whole world had faded into a kind of pale, soupy, grayish monochrome.

"Ma'am?" Nori turned in the doorway of Malloy's Mercantile. Back at the cash register, the checkout girl was waving Nori's plastic bag of purchases. "Don't forget your bag."

Nori retraced her steps and made an effort to smile as she took the proffered bag. As she walked away she made some comment about forgetting her head if it wasn't attached.

She had purchased a package of flimsy, cheap towels that might make good rags, plus a six-pack of heavy, wool work socks. In her former life, Nori never wore this kind of footwear. Her city socks were mostly light trouser ones that she wore underneath dress pants. Sometimes at home she would put on funky socks with flowers or diamond patterns. After a few weeks of blisters here at Whisper Lake though, she decided she needed something heavier inside her work boots.

Before she reached her truck she stopped and counted, just in case. One—Malloy's Mercantile bag, two—shoulder bag, three—sunglasses, four—cell phone. Keys? In pocket. She threw the plastic shopping bag on the passenger seat and grabbed her backpack, which contained her laptop, closed the truck door, aimed the remote and locked it, and off she went to Marlene's Café.

Grief and stress, she told herself. What had

everyone told her? Don't make any major life changes for a year? Well, maybe in her case eighteen months wasn't long enough. Stress and grief were making her forget things. Like packages.

Stress and grief were turning her into a loony woman, a crazy sleepwalker. She was nowhere near over mourning Marty. She should have realized that because sometime during the night she had sleepwalked herself into her kitchen and opened up her cupboard doors and left them that way.

This morning when she woke, she had felt marvelous. She'd had a long night of uninterrupted dreamless sleep. It was rare for her to sleep that soundly and for so long. Maybe it was knowing that she finally had someone who would work for her that allowed her to rest. The sun was shining and the day was promising to be lovely and warm. Today, she would face her fears of the storm and go back out in the kayak. Today, she might even mount the steps into her loft and get out her paints.

Nori was a muralist. Essentially, she painted what people told her to, which was mostly humongous scenes of old country towns on the sides of buildings. It was her work and she loved it. Yet since Marty died, she hadn't touched a paintbrush. She just couldn't bring herself to. It was like that part of her—the artist part—had died with him.

But today, with the sun streaming into her window and leaving ribbons of gold on her walls, it would be different. She would paint. Today would be the day when she would get back to being an artist. It had been too long.

After she had woken up this morning, she had gone into her kitchen. The cupboards next to the sink were wide-open and the cups she and Steve had drunk coffee in yesterday were up on the shelf. She had stared, perplexed. She hadn't remembered putting them there. She had left them in the sink. Hadn't she? And how had she left the cupboard door open?

She was always fastidious about keeping her cupboards closed. Marty was the one who was forever leaving them open and when she would complain, he would take her in his arms, dance around the kitchen and say, "Ah, my little Elnora." And he would push her hair off her face and plant a kiss on her mouth.

She would playfully push him away and say, "You know, that's not going to get you anywhere, and don't call me Elnora. That's my grand-mother's name. My name is Nori." And she would one by one close the cupboards, making a point of doing so.

When she went to close the cupboards, some-thing way in the back caught her eye. A bit of color. She reached for it. It was a tiny bell. It looked to be a cream-colored china bell with a decorative hand-painted purple flower on one side.

She rang it. It had a pretty tinkling sound. Had this been in here the whole time? And how was it that she hadn't seen it before? Or maybe she hadn't looked in the farthest reaches of her cupboard. That had to be it.

She told herself that she was still so disorganized from her unpacking, it could've been here the whole time and she wouldn't have seen it.

She experimented with the cupboard door. She closed it hard and it bounced back open. There. That's all that was. The latches were broken. Steve's new cupboards would be a great improvement.

She had taken the bell into the living room and placed it on the mantel. Off the kitchen there was a large room that was loaded with boxes of antiques, junk, dressers and trunks. That's where the Shaker rocker had come from. Perhaps there were more bells like this in that room.

Pushing thoughts of the cupboard doors out of her mind, she entered Marlene's café. Selena was her waitress this morning. She was a tall, thin, pretty girl with long, straight, brown hair. Yet, despite her innate prettiness, she always seemed hollow eyed and haunted, as if she bore the cares of the world. Nori had been told that Selena had graduated from high school last year, but wanted some time off before she decided what she wanted to do with her life.

"Hello, Mrs. Edwards," the girl said. "Would you like a menu?"

"Just coffee would be great."

"I'll get you some milk."

"Thanks." Nori preferred milk to cream in her coffee and a lot of restaurants only served cream. But Nori had been coming here so often that they knew her preferences.

A few minutes later Selena returned with a little pitcher. Nori's laptop was already open.

Her first e-mail was from her daughter Daphne. Even though Daphne and Rachel were identical twins, they were miles apart in temperament. Daphne was vocal and articulate. She typically wrote long e-mails, detailing everything they did at camp—from waking in the morning until the lights went out at night. Nori read it eagerly. Daphne went on about the new friends they had made, the awesome worship band, and the cute guy who played drums. Nori wrote long, chatty, happy-faced e-mails to her daughters at camp.

You'll love it here. It's so beautiful . . .

You wouldn't believe the mouse droppings I've had to clean out . . .

And the bugs! I've never seen such big spiders . . .

And you should see the guy I've hired to work on the place. He's huge! You know your Uncle Phil? He's even bigger than Uncle Phil . . .

She paused, her fingers on the keyboard, and allowed herself to think about Steve for a while.

What idiocy had been a part of her brain when she said her daughters could go off and work June and July at a Christian camp? She thought back to their mother-daughter times, holding on to one another all night that first night after Marty died. Then more recently, watching videos, eating popcorn, shopping and all the things they did. Just the three of them. She missed them so much now.

She was finishing up reading her last e-mail when Marlene came and took a seat across from her and asked her how everything was going.

"You will be happy to know that I finally got someone to work out at Trail's End for me," Nori said. "I think you know him."

"Great!" Marlene placed her hands flat on the table. "Steve Baylor?"

She nodded.

Marlene cheered. "Well, I'm glad he finally took my advice. Roy and I told him to come see you. Now we can take you off the prayer line."

Prayer line? "He seems like a nice guy," Nori said.

"He is. A very nice guy. He's had a bit of a hard go of things, though."

Despite herself, Nori was interested.

Marlene continued, "We get the story at church sometimes. He has a son he never sees. We sometimes pray for him in our small group."

"He told me about him."

Marlene folded her hands. Her fingernails were long and red. She wore a lot of rings. "Well, I'm glad he opened up. The Steven Baylor I know is a bit reticent. It's hard for him to open up to people."

"Maybe I caught him in a mood." Nori pulled a chunk of hair away from her face for a moment and remembered Steve's face as they had knelt close together beside her fireplace. "Has his son ever been here?" Nori wondered.

Marlene said, "Just once that I remember. Jeffrey is a cute little gaffer. You should see him. Big. Like Steve. Big for his age."

"It's sad they don't get to see each other more often."

"It is. I feel so sorry for the little tyke. And for Steve. Steve came to the Crossing after his divorce three years ago and went into business for himself."

"What did he do before that?"

"I don't know exactly. Government work is what he says. I presume he was some sort of carpenter for the government. He and Alec are friends. Sometimes he works with Alec. Steve must be some sort of auxiliary police officer here."

"Who's Alec?" Nori asked.

"He's the sheriff. You haven't met him, I guess." Nori shook her head.

"You will."

While they talked, her e-mail icon flashed. "Oh," Nori said, clicking on the icon. "I just got some pictures of Daphne and Rachel. Here, let me show you my girls." She moved her computer screen around the table so Marlene could see.

"My goodness, your daughters are such pretty things." She said it loudly. "Selena!" Everything about Marlene was big, from her blond curls to her voice to her mannerisms. "Selena, come, sweetie, and have look at the pictures of Daphne and Rachel."

The way she said *Daphne and Rachel* cheered Nori. It was like she was referring to old friends, kids already a part of the community. This would be a good place for her girls, she was sure of it.

But Selena didn't come over. Instead, she kept her back turned to her mother and put a new coffee filter into the commercial coffeemaker.

Marlene's face was blank as she watched her daughter for a moment. Nori didn't know what she would do if one of her daughters blatantly ignored her like that, but Marlene simply turned back to Nori and said quietly, "I try to excuse Selena. The kids here have all been through a bit of a bad patch."

"What happened?" Nori asked.

Marlene lowered her voice.

"About a year ago one of the very popular girls went missing. It's been hard on all of them. Especially Selena. She and Heather were close."

"Went missing?" Nori took a sip of her coffee. "What do you mean?"

"Disappeared. Gone. Heather was a sweet girl.

She was quite active in the church youth group. Poor Heather, as sometimes happens, she got in with the wrong crowd. Phyllis, that's Heather's mother, and I used to have long talks. Anyway, she got herself some boyfriend from Bangor and the two disappeared. No one's seen or heard from them since. Phyllis has never lost hope that her daughter is alive somewhere, but I think Alec—" she lowered her voice to practically a whisper "— believes they both came to foul play." She paused, letting her words sink in.

Nori said. "That's horrible! Both of them?" She had no idea that something like this could happen in so lovely a place.

Marlene nodded, then glanced back at Selena's stiff back.

The bell over the door at Marlene's Café jingled as a few more customers entered.

"Well," Marlene said, raising her bulk out of the chair. "Duty calls. That's why I try to give Selena the benefit of the doubt every now and then."

A few minutes later, Nori closed her laptop and got up to leave. As she exited the café she glanced up at Selena, who was leaning into the counter. "Have a nice day, Selena," she said.

But the girl merely hugged a stack of menus into her chest and looked at Nori with dark and frightened eyes as if she was hiding some deep and dreadful secret.

THREE

Nori knew that losing someone special takes its toll. She knew how difficult losing Marty had been on the girls. Losing a best friend and not even knowing whether that friend was dead or alive would be especially horrid.

She glanced at the clock in the truck's console. Ten thirty-five. Steve had said he would be out at Trail's End after lunch, if he was able to get all of his supplies and organize a work party. It could take a day, he had told her, to get a crew and materials ready.

She decided to head home and maybe begin clearing the beach. Or maybe she would go through the junk in the room out back or unpack more of her own boxes. She made a mental list as she drove. She would work inside this morning, unpacking more, then this afternoon in the sun, she'd tackle the waterfront.

Scrub trees and weeds grew in tangles down to the water's edge. She wanted to clear away the underbrush and see what she was dealing with in terms of a beach. There was an enormous, perfectly formed fir tree near the run-down dock. That would remain, but much of the rest would go. She wanted to keep the whole place as natural as she could, but she also recognized that guests wouldn't be comfortable hiking through boggy weeds and leech-filled marshes to get to the lake. She was currently studying a book on green water spaces that was giving her lots of ideas. She also needed a new dock. That would be another thing she would talk to Steve about.

So lost was she in thought that she didn't immediately realize it when she found herself on an unfamiliar street. It didn't particularly worry her, however. She wasn't lost. It was pretty much impossible to get lost in Whisper Lake Crossing. The place just wasn't that big. Whisper Lake Crossing, or as the locals simply called it, the Crossing, had one main street called, uniquely enough, Main Street. It housed most of the businesses in town—Malloy's Mercantile, a drugstore, Earl's Gas and Convenience, a video rental place, a hair salon, a few other retail shops and coffee shops, including Marlene's Café; a Chinese restaurant, a deli, plus a smattering of antique and gift shops. Many of the shops shut down in the winter. A lot of them had already opened up for the summer. The nearest big grocery store was nine miles away in Shawnigan.

Instead of making an immediate U-turn when she realized her mistake, Nori kept on going. Up ahead she was losing the pavement. Like most of the roads in the Crossing, this one turned into gravel. This road ran beside the lake, but she was going in the very opposite direction than she should be. She knew Trail's End was across the lake somewhere, but not likely visible from this end. Still, she kept on. It was pretty here with the lake to the right of her. Such a pretty area to be marred by tragedy.

She was about to turn around and go back when a large, well-kept home with a sign out front caught her eye—Whisper Lake Museum and Historical Society. The grounds out front boasted well-tended flower gardens and a neatly mowed lawn. Early in the summer the beds blossomed with color. Farm implements were arranged artfully on the grass and a stylized sign announced the hours: Monday—Wednesday, 9–1. Summer Hours, Monday—Saturday, 9-5. Summer hours began in another two weeks, she noted.

Today, however was Tuesday. She turned into the driveway, her tires crackling over the gravel. Maybe it was time she learned a bit about the history of Trail's End.

The small visitors' parking lot out front was empty except for a dark green Volvo. Nori pulled in beside it, and wondered if this place ever got any tourists. Probably the only visitors were die-hard historians who researched genealogies or obscure histories, the kind of people who carried notebooks and tromped through graveyards.

She walked up the steps and onto a newly painted wraparound porch. A couple of oversize Cape Cod chairs faced each other in amongst hanging flower baskets of variegated petunias.

A breeze with an edge of coolness blew her hair across her face as she read the sign on the front door—Welcome! Come right in!

She pushed open the door, which set off a series of tinkling bells. Despite the sound, which was jarring and sonorous, no one greeted her. She seemed to be alone in the place. It was dim and the first thing she noticed was a chill in the air, like a cave. She blinked, waited. No one came. When her eyes adjusted to the light, she looked around.

Walls were covered with displays and it smelled faintly of musty books and lemon oil. It reminded her of an old liturgical church—full of books and robes and lemon-polished wood.

The wall along the left was done up like a hundred-year-old apothecary. Behind a long customer shelf were open cupboards with row upon row of tiny glass bottles. Next to them were rolls of cloth, small wooden boxes of pins and old-fashioned baking instruments.

It was the sort of place, she thought, where people could donate their rusting, ancient farm implements, cooking pots and books. She thought about all the stuff at her place. Maybe when she got that storeroom organized she could bring some of the stuff here.

On the other side of the room were shelves and glass display cabinets. One of the displays was a series of readers used in the Whisper Lake Crossing one-room schoolhouse. Nori went from one exhibit to the next. It was all very interesting, but wasn't what she was looking for.

The whole place was deathly quiet, and Nori felt as if she had gone through some portal and been transported to a place a hundred years ago.

At the very back of the room Nori found a wall-board that looked to be a timeline history of the area. Nori studied picture after picture and read caption after caption, yet found nothing about her cabins or anything pertaining to Trail's End. She became conscious then of someone behind her and slightly to her left; someone simply standing there, unmoving, a tall woman. Out of the corner of her eye she saw that the woman's hands were clasped in front of her and that she was dressed in period clothing. An instant later, Nori realized it was a mannequin, but not before she had turned to say hello.

"I see you've met Mildred," a voice called from the other side of the room. A small, compact women with fluffy white hair made her way toward Nori. Around her shoulders she clutched a paisley scarf that looked too large for her small frame.

"She startled me is all," Nori said. "I was con-centrating on the display."

"Mildred startles everybody. I keep telling her to stay put in her room, but she just won't listen. She insists on coming out and greeting our visitors." The woman laughed easily, and Nori relaxed in her presence.

The woman went on, "Mildred was a gift from the mercantile. We thought we could use her here at the museum. The schoolkids love her. You should read some of the letters we get addressed to 'Dear Mildred.'"

"I bet," said Nori.

The woman came toward her. "Where are my manners? I'm Bette. I volunteer here a few mornings a week."

"It's nice to meet you. I'm Nori Edwards. I'm new to the area."

"You must be the woman who bought Trail's End."

"You know about me?"

"My son will be working out there with Steve."

"Oh."

Bette was pleasant and Nori thought her British accent was quite quaint among all these Mainers and their drawls.

"You will love it here. I guarantee it," Bette said. "This is a lovely little community. The locals are a bit reserved in some aspects, but I've been here for many years, and I would never live anywhere else. People said I was crazy to move here, but I've proved them all wrong."

Nori nodded.

Bette continued. "The lake really grows on you. In my opinion, this is the perfect climate. Oh, the winters can be a bit much, but the springs are lovely and the summers are not too hot. But it is the autumns that are magnificent. That is the time of year when you get to see what an extraordinary artist God is. Sorry, I do go on. You'll have to forgive me."

"It's okay," Nori said.

Bette put her hand on Nori's arm and Nori found herself warming to the woman. "Trail's End is lovely," Bette said. "In many respects it's the most beautiful spot on the entire Whisper Lake. I think you'll be happy there."

Nori said, "It is beautiful. But I'm wondering if you would have any historical information about Trail's End."

"Trail's End. We might have a little bit." She wrapped her shawl around her more securely. "You folks have really taken on a lot. I hope your husband is a handyman."

"My husband is . . . not with me."

"Oh, I'm sorry. Steve didn't tell me anything about your situation. Just that he would be working out there."

"It's okay," Nori said again.

After a pause, Bette said, "I came here with my young son. It's just been the two of us for almost as long as I can remember. We have a bit of a guest home, nothing quite so grand as Trail's End. We have four cottages that we rent. I've done it on my own. I'm sure you can, too."

Nori said, "I have two daughters who will be coming out at the end of the summer to help. I have all these ideas of turning it into a kind of retreat center."

Nori found herself telling Bette about Daphne and Rachel and her plans for Trail's End. Bette was full of questions and ideas, and when they had finally exhausted the subject, the older woman said something that startled her. "I'm sure the locals have told you about the resident ghost?"

Nori stared openmouthed at the woman.

Bette's eyes flickered at Nori's surprise. "Some people in this community really go off the deep end when it comes to ghosts and hauntings at the lake. I mean even the name Whisper Lake is said to be named for the fact that you can hear the whispers of ghosts across it. But those of us who know better are really trying to downplay that part of our history."

Nori bit her lip.

"I may have a book somewhere. Oh, yes. Probably in the back. Come with me. That seems to be Whisper Lake's only claim to fame. Which totally infuriates me and most other people here in Whisper Lake Crossing."

Nori followed her into an office in the back where Bette rummaged through a bookshelf. "I think all of this renewed interest in ghosts may be attributed to that television documentary."

"What documentary?" Nori was curious.

"A year or so ago one of those unsolved ghost sightings television programs came out here to film this place, as well as your place." The woman shook her head as she rummaged through the bookshelf. "And my goodness. Wouldn't you know it? This is the only book I have on your place. Well . . ." She placed the book on the table. "You can read about the history of the first inhabitants of Trail's End, but ignore the ghost thing."

The title on the cover of the book was *The Ghost of Whisper Lake.* The cover picture was a reproduction of an old tinplate photograph of a young woman who was dressed in woodsmen's clothing—dark wool breeches and a buckskin jacket. Her black hair was pulled back and up in some sort of plait or bun behind her head, although Nori couldn't tell from the picture. Unsecured bits of hair wisped around her face. It looked curly, and Nori touched her own hair, which waved of its own accord, too.

A long rifle was in her right hand, butt on the ground. She held the barrel of it without smiling.

Nori wanted to keep gazing at this picture, at this woman—there was something about her—but Bette flipped to a center section of glossy photographic plates. The first was one of the lodge, although devoid of the loft and its windows, which gave it so much character. The lodge without the loft looked like nothing more than a large rugged hunting cabin, like the ones along the shore that she regularly kayaked beside, only bigger.

The overgrown beach was cleared of brush and it looked like there was actually sand there. There was no dock, but several long canoes were pulled up on the shoreline.

Nori found herself wondering about this woman. Had she, like Nori, come out here by herself to live? Was there some great sadness in her life that had made her come here? What was her story?

As if to answer that question, Bette turned the page to a black-and-white photo of a couple. "Her name was Molly Jones. She and her husband, James, homesteaded. They cleared the land and built Trail's End lodge. The cabins were added later. I wish I had more books on Molly and James. I know the Bangor Public Library does though."

Nori was fascinated by the pictures of her lodge and property. She even recognized some of the trees, smaller then. She looked back at the couple.

"They were in their early twenties," Bette said. "She's apparently the ghost. Don't know how these old legends get started. Molly was the ghost, not James, although James had the more violent death."

"What happened to them?" Nori asked, her finger on the picture of Molly Jones.

"Molly and James were out checking their traplines when James was attacked and killed by a bear. Molly was able to shoot the bear, but not before James died.

"After James died, Molly stayed on by herself. She loved the place and decided she couldn't leave." Bette opened to another picture. "She and James hand-built those canoes you see there on the shore. The story is that one day Molly took a canoe out onto the lake when one of our famous storms came up. She never made it back. Storms can be vicious on this lake, thunderstorms, especially. All that anyone found was her overturned canoe floating along the shores off Twin Peaks Island. Her body was never recovered."

Nori shuddered. She couldn't help it. She was remembering the lightning flashing all around her on the lake yesterday.

"They never found her?" she finally asked.

Bette shook her head. "And that's not for lack of trying. People still come here looking for her. According to legend, if they find her bones she'll stop haunting the place. Quite a story I would say."

"Can I borrow the book?"

"Sure. Although I'd be surprised if there wasn't a copy on your property someplace."

Nori chuckled. "No doubt there is. I've got a storeroom filled with junk."

Nori made her way out to her truck, the book pressed against her chest. She wanted to head right home and dive into the reading of it, but she remembered that she needed shampoo and hair conditioner at the drugstore.

She parked on Main Street and soon found the things she was looking for. She got in line behind Joe from Earl's Convenience. She said hello to the young man, but Joe barely acknowledged her presence. He kept his head down. That seemed to be the story with all the young people she'd met here. And now she knew why. Joe was picking up a prescription, she saw. Even though she had bought Trail's End from his father, she'd never formally met Earl, just his two sons, Chase and Joe, where she bought her gas.

Behind her was a voice she recognized. It was the man known as Peach. "Rumor has it that you're going to be digging up the place out there, putting in condos and the like," Peach said to her.

Nori laughed. "I wish!"

Joe brushed past her with his little prescription bag and his head still down. Peach said, "That for Earl?"

Joe nodded, tight-lipped.

When Joe was out of sight, Peach whispered, "Earl has a bad back. Fell when he was working out at Trail's End. Up on a roof of one of the cabins and he slipped right off. Hasn't been the same since. That's why he had to sell."

"That's too bad."

"Pretty much addicted to all them drugs, he is."

Nori didn't say anything, just dismissed him as a gossipy old man.

When she got in her car she looked down into

the face of Molly Jones next to her in the passenger seat. She stared for a moment. It looked as if the woman on the cover of the book was looking directly up at her, as if this Molly Jones had something she wanted to tell her.

Steve enjoyed the feel of smooth wood. He liked the smell of it as he ran his grandfather's plane on it smoothing the rough edges. He liked the soft hiss as he ran his sandpaper over the contours. It was almost hypnotic. Taking a rough piece of wood with its corduroy grain and creating something polished and functional and strong was satisfying. It was like making order out of chaos. He wished he could do the same in his own life— smooth away the damaged edges, sand away all the confused questions.

He wished it was this easy to sand away twenty years of military service. Soldiers on ordinary rounds suffered post-traumatic stress. How much worse was his, with the things he'd been forced to do, the things he'd seen, all in the name of defense of one's country.

Sometimes at night when the images came, he had to close his eyes and pray. And pray. And pray.

That's why he loved woodwork—you could make order out of chaos. He continued to sand the chair.

The leg that had splintered yesterday with dry rot had been replaced once, he saw, by cheap pine.

A poor choice for long-term wear. He had a piece of oak that was just about the same size and width. This would be perfect.

Another thing he would replace was the webbing on the seat itself. Not only had he broken the chair leg when he fell, he had also gone through the cracked and rotting cloth. He would replace this with leather secured with grommets, or strips of wood that he would heat and bend over the frame.

He was still embarrassed when he thought about falling right through Nori's chair and onto her floor. Humiliated because there he was, sprawled on the floor, but also chagrined because he—who knew and loved old chairs—should have known you don't sit on old chairs without checking.

He took a moment to look through the one window in his workshop. A wooded trail ended a short distance away at the lake. He could see the lake through the trees. Chester lay sprawled in the doorway.

Steve loved his workshop. He had morphed this outbuilding into a place where he could escape. It was one of the places he felt most at home. He liked the solitude of it. A lot of people who did what he did—his father for example—kept music on all day. When he was a boy he always knew when his father was working. The classical music blasted through the house from his dad's basement wood workshop.

Steve, on the other hand, preferred quiet, the birds in the summer, the sounds of the falling snow in the winter, the scratchy hiss of the sandpaper.

When he'd gotten home last night, he'd taken the chair immediately to his workshop, and then, because he couldn't help himself, he'd worked on this grand old chair until the wee hours. He'd gotten up early and headed out here. "So, Chester," Steve said, holding the beginning of the chair leg up to the light. "What do you think?"

His dog raised one ear, clearly unimpressed. Maybe—if he would admit it to himself—today it was to take his mind off Nori. But it wasn't working. Since yesterday his mind seemed to have been stuck on Nori like a scratched CD.

Nori Edwards was *married*. He had seen the picture. He had seen the ring.

He placed the new chair leg on his workbench. She was off-limits and he, of all people, should understand about that. Yet there she stayed, right in the forefront of his thinking, no matter how many times he tried to pray her away. So he prayed for her. He prayed that whatever her situation, whatever the particular sadness that marred her face, she would find peace.

Chester was up now, standing in the doorway, looking toward the lake and wagging his tail.

"What's out there, pal? Squirrel?"

Some moments later, Steve heard the car. He

wiped his sawdusty hands on his jeans and went out into the bright and blinding sunshine. He wasn't the least surprised to see Alec, the sheriff, open his car door and get out. Chester made a bee-line toward him.

"I've been wondering when you were going to show up," Steve said walking out toward him.

Alec and Chester had a good friendship, mainly because Alec always carried a pocketful of dog treats with him wherever he went.

"So what are you working on in here?" Alec asked, changing the subject.

"A Shaker chair. A rocker. Come on in. I'll show you. One of the legs broke. I've already got a replacement started. Plus, the seat."

"Nice." Alec made his way into the shop and looked at Steve's handiwork. "Where'd you get it?"

"Trail's End," Steve said.

Alec nodded.

"Which is why you're here," Steve said. "As I said, I'm not surprised."

"News travels. I was just at Marlene's."

Alec was probably Steve's closest friend. Only Alec knew the full extent of Steve's résumé, that Steve had been a Special Operative with the military. The most that people in Whisper Lake Crossing knew was that Steve had "worked for the government." Locals assumed he'd been some sort of carpenter for the government. He didn't correct them. It was easier to have only a few people know.

"You want coffee? I got some in the pot." Steve pointed to a dust-covered pot half-filled with dark liquid and perched on a shelf.

"Knowing it's probably sat there since dawn, I'll pass."

"You could always make new."

"That I could." Alec went over and was about to dump the old coffee into a deep metal sink, when Steve put up his hand.

"Wait, let me finish it off. No sense wasting it."

Alec shook his head and Steve poured the rest of the viscous liquid into an oversize mug that read: *Maine, the way life should be.*

"Don't know how you can drink that stuff," Alec said.

"It's called watching my pennies."

"So when do you begin out there?" Alec asked.

"Tomorrow morning. First thing. None of my crew can start until then, but that gives me time to get to Shawnigan and get a few supplies. I'll be going there soon."

Alec poured water into the reservoir and spooned in new coffee. "Who do you have working for you?" The coffee began dripping through. Its aroma filled the small room.

"So far, Chase and Ralph. I'm trying to persuade Connolly. He's a good worker. I've worked with him before. Plus, I'm hoping to round up a few of the kids from the youth group for cleanup. She could sure use it. Who is that girl with the red spikes in her black hair—short hair?" Steve motioned with his hand.

"That would be Blaine."

"Blaine. Yes. I should remember her name."

"You should. We interviewed them all at great length."

Steven raised his eyebrows and did remember. "Also, that tall friend of hers who's always with Blaine—Meredith."

"Kids won't want to go out there."

"I know."

"So you'll have a look around there? I know that's why you took the job."

His friend knew him well. And if Steve could admit it to himself, that was precisely why he went out there yesterday. He and Alec had worked hard on that case, and had been able to find exactly—nothing.

Steve took a long swallow of old coffee. Pretty bad. Maybe he'd wait for the new brew. In the four years that Trail's End had remained unsold, it had been used by young people for bush parties. The police regularly made weekend trips out there to break up the parties or fights.

Fifteen months ago a local girl, Heather Malloy, went missing along with her boyfriend, Scott Gramble. For weeks her frantic parents assumed she and Scott, a boy from Bangor no one seemed to know, had run off together. A message left on her Facebook pointed in that direction.

Heather and Scott are enjoying a new life! We've decided to go away, and by the time anyone reads this, we'll be happy and together.

The police were able to trace the Facebook message back to Selena's computer. When confronted, Selena seemed genuinely surprised and said that sometimes Heather used her computer at school. She really had no other explanation. The Bangor police were never able to track the boyfriend down. All they had was a name, Scott Gramble, and a bit of a description. Multiple searches of Grambles throughout the entire northeast yielded nothing.

For three months no one knew that all the kids, including Heather and Scott, had been to a party out at Trail's End. None of them would talk about it. Finally, a girl named Meredith let it slip that they had all been out there with Heather and Scott. It was determined that this was the last time she had been seen by anyone. Selena finally admitted to Alec that they hadn't come forward sooner because they knew they weren't supposed to be there. Plus, the party had occurred after a church sponsored youth event.

The party attendees included Chase, Joe, Selena, Connolly, Blaine and Meredith. They were rounded up and interviewed individually. All of them were tight-lipped. A few said they had remembered seeing Heather and Scott at the party, while others shook their heads and said they hadn't.

To Steve's trained eye, they seemed afraid and even his gentlest, friendliest methods of interrogation—learned from long years in the military—yielded nothing but silence.

Rumors flew. Everything from the couple was happy and living in Canada, to Scott murdered Heather and threw her body in the lake and now roamed the woods behind Trail's End like a crazy person; to someone murdered both Heather and Scott and buried their bodies at Trail's End. The word *ghost* had begun to be spoken in hushed tones whenever anyone mentioned Trail's End. Even though many people had lived there quite happily and uneventfully through the years, suddenly everyone was talking about the ghost of Molly Jones. Earl's fall off the cabin roof was suddenly called "mysterious."

Alec still believed that the mystery of the teenagers' disappearance lay somewhere at Trail's End, and so did Steve. Alec poured himself a cup of coffee and sat down on a folding chair, leaned the back against the wall and said, "I'm thinking of asking the new owner if we can have a look around."

"That would be Nori Edwards."

"She married?"

Steve nodded, and was quiet for a minute before he answered, "But she's by herself out there."

Alec brought his chair down so that the front legs were on the ground. He said, "Do you think this Nori Edwards might know something? Could she be related to Scott Gramble? Did you get the impression she knew anything? Why she's there?"

Steve scratched Chester's ears before he said, "She didn't strike me as knowing much about Trail's End."

Alec said, "I still may look into her, check her out. Just to be sure of what we're dealing with."

"She's got two daughters. Twins. Her fireplace mantel is covered with photos." Steve felt a pang when he thought about the two girls, their arms around their smiling father.

"Anybody can put up a few framed photos and call it a family," Alec said.

Steve shot him a look and said, "I'll have a look around. That's all I can promise. But my best guess is that she's not involved."

"Let's just see."

He took another long drink of his coffee. And wondered. How was he so sure that Nori Edwards was who she said she was?

On her way out of town Nori rummaged through her bag until she found the business card Steve had given her. She needed to touch base, make sure he had enough kids to work, and ask him if they'd be coming this afternoon or tomorrow.

When she got him on the phone he told her he'd spent time on her chair. He was organizing a work party, but most of the teenagers couldn't start until the following day. "I decided to head into Shawnigan to have a look at wood and counter-tops for your kitchen. I'll get a bunch of samples for you to look at."

"How about if I go with you?" She slowed her truck to a stop. She had just turned onto the six-mile gravel road to Trail's End. "I could meet you in Shawnigan. Just tell me where."

"I'm in Whisper Lake. Why don't we meet in town and travel together? No need to take two vehicles."

They agreed. She'd park her truck behind Marlene's Café and go with him.

The ride into Shawnigan took fifteen minutes, during which time Steve mostly told her what he was doing with the rocking chair.

When they arrived in Shawnigan, she followed him through lumberyards and showrooms, looking at wood and countertop samples. She wanted a lighter wood, while he tried to convince her that darker wood would be better for so large a kitchen. "It would give it class," he said.

"I trust your judgment," she finally told him, and chose one halfway between the light one she had originally looked at on the Web and the darker wood that he was recommending.

She tagged along to another hardware store and watched him pick through some wood files and other tools. "For the chair," he explained.

"I'm glad you've been able to spend so much time on it."

"It's a beautiful chair. I hope I can do it justice."

"I'm sure you can."

They were there at noon and ended up eating a fast-food lunch at a picnic table behind a place that overlooked the lake. Between bites of her fish sandwich she asked him what he had done before he moved here.

He was thoughtful for a while. He didn't say anything, just stared away from her and out at the lake. After a long silence he said, "Government work."

"What did you do for the government?"

"Boring stuff. Nothing special."

The way he shrugged made her feel as if this was a place he didn't want to go. She'd respect that. Everyone had secret places.

He put his ham sandwich down on his napkin and looked at it. There were squint lines around his eyes. He rubbed the side of his nose with his forefinger. His nose looked slightly crooked, almost as if it had been broken. She wondered about that. He seemed to see where her gaze had landed and scratched the side of it self-consciously.

She picked up her soda and took a drink although she wasn't particularly thirsty. She put it down, wiped her mouth with her napkin, all while Steve turned his gaze back out on a sailboater on the lake. She got the idea that he'd been hurt badly in life. Maybe it was when his wife left with his son.

At one point during their lunch their hands touched and he drew back as if burned. As they returned to the truck, he kept his distance.

It occurred to her on the quiet way home that they had spent the past two hours together and, aside from her one question about his former employment, all they had talked about was woods and stains and doors and chairs and countertop styles.

Nori sat in the passenger seat and twisted her wedding band. She saw him look at her doing this. Probably he was wondering why a widow would wear her wedding ring for so long after her husband had died. She wanted to tell him why she still wore it, that taking it off would be so final.

"Would you like some licorice?" he asked.

"What?" The question was unexpected.

"Licorice," he said, and pulled a package of red candy from his jacket pocket. "I bought it back at the gas station." He laid it on the dashboard between them.

The package was crinkled from being in his pocket. He tore off a strip and chewed on a hunk.

"You like licorice?" She looked at him curiously.

"Love it," he said. "Help yourself."

She did so. How many years had it been since she had eaten red licorice? She broke off a piece and thought about amusement parks at the shore, sharing pieces of candy with her girlfriends as they walked the grounds in search of friends.

"It's good, isn't it?" he said, looking at her with a half grin. "Takes you back, doesn't it?"

"It does."

He said, "I never outgrew my love for this stuff."

"Your dentist must love you," Nori said. She looked at his hands as they held the steering wheel. Strong hands. Despite his outdoor work, his nails were neatly cut and clean.

"I was blessed with good teeth," he added.

"How about chocolate?" Nori asked.

"Take it or leave it."

"Me, too," she said.

He gave her that crooked, wide smile again. "Really? I thought all women liked chocolate."

"I'm not all women."

"I can see that. Here." He pushed the package toward her across the dashboard. "Put the rest in your pocket for later." He grabbed his cell phone and attached his hands-free. "I have another food question. Have you had a chance to sample Selena's potpies?"

"You go from licorice to potpies . . ."

He grinned again. "I guess I like food."

She watched his expressive mouth.

"Marlene has given her the run of the place when it comes to pastry. She's been out of high school a year, and everyone thinks she's going to go into baking, or cooking. Marlene told me this morning that Selena was making potpies today."

"Really? How nice." Why was he telling her this? she wondered.

"I'm putting in an order for a beef one for myself. She makes beef, chicken and vegetarian. You want me to get one for you while I'm at it? You can put it in your fridge for later. My treat."

His treat? "Um. Maybe chicken."

He punched the number into his cell phone and she listened while he ordered one beef pie. "And one chicken. Make this extra special. Nori Edwards hasn't sampled your pies, so make it a good introduction."

He was buying her pie? And grinning at her? Was this a date? Why was she feeling so uneasy?

FOUR

When Nori got home her door was unlocked. She stood on her porch, packages, laptop and chicken pie in hand and puzzled over this. She was sure she had locked it.

She grasped at her collar and looked around her in the late-afternoon sun. Such a peaceful place. Not a soul in sight. Just the birds and the occasional squirrel. The lake was an emerald in the slanting rays of the sun. She was totally alone out here. And the suddenness of that thought almost left her breathless. But this was what she wanted, wasn't it? To get away from the city and start a new life? To make a new home in the woods? Safe in the woods? Then why did she feel this panic? She whirled, faced the woods and that's when she saw the tiny bell perched on her porch railing.

The bell? How did it get out here? She had taken the bell into the living room and placed it on the mantel. That, she was certain of. She went to it and looked it over. It wasn't the same one. This one was pale blue with a yellow flower on the side. The clapper was larger and the sound it made was more sonorous. She closed her hand around the bell and for the briefest of seconds she was filled with a kind of horror. She twirled around and looked in every direction, but all she saw was stillness and peace.

The terrifying moment passed. She was being silly, of course. Probably someone had left it here for her. Bette from the museum. Yes, that's what had happened. This morning she had asked Bette for information about the bell. And then Bette had found one, brought it out and left it on her porch. Most likely there had been a note attached and it had blown away in the breeze.

She left her parcels by the door and walked around her porch, certain she would see a note on the ground in front. There was nothing, but that didn't mean anything, right? It could have blown farther. Or maybe Bette forgot to leave a note.

And the door being unlocked? Simple explanation. She had forgotten to lock it. Ever since Marty had died she hadn't been herself. She knew this. She was more stressed than she knew. She was more stressed than she even felt.

Once inside, she went around and locked all the doors and windows. And then she double-checked everything. She put the kettle on for tea and sat down at the kitchen table with the book about Molly Jones and the chicken pie. The ghost of Molly Jones. It's no wonder that ghost myths abounded. You forget to lock your door and suddenly your first thought is ghosts. Silly, she told herself as she looked at the front of the book.

Molly Jones's skin was dewy, flawless. She looked no older than Rachel or Daphne as she stood there holding that huge gun.

Nori decided to skim through the book quickly at first and then go back and study each chapter word for word. She grabbed a fork and, even though it was only midafternoon, she found herself enjoying the chicken as she read about Molly's early years. The book began with Molly and James in New York state. Molly and James had gone to the same one-room school, and when she was sixteen and he was seventeen they married. Three years later they decided to homestead. They came by canoe across the body of water known as Black Lake to investigate pieces of property.

Nori read how they had transported all of their possessions and building materials by a horse-drawn sleigh from the town site—now Whisper Lake Crossing—in February when the lake was frozen. They built a small cabin and Molly called the place Trail's End.

Nori ate more pie as she read:

It was Molly who changed the name from Black Lake to Whisper Lake. She was the one who first laid claim to the fact that a person could hear whispers when the wind came in from the northwest. As a result, the town known as Pine Crossing came to be known as Whisper Lake Crossing. She claimed they were the whispers of everyone who had died while caught out on the lake in storms.

Nori shuddered and glanced through the window at the smooth emerald lake. She skimmed through chapters full of how they spent their days—chopping wood, trapping, building. Skim. Skim. Skim. She breezed through an entire chapter on how to churn butter. Skim some more. She slowed abruptly when she came to the part about James's death. She read with renewed horror how Molly had shot the bear that ultimately killed her husband.

She turned the page and read:

After James's death, Molly decided to stay on. Trail's End became to her a kind of sanctuary, a place where she could be alone with her thoughts and with her art. She began painting at this time, and became known for her exquisite miniature watercolors.

Molly was an artist!

On the next page was a black-and-white reproduction of one of her paintings. It was the tiny red flowers that grew along the path Nori had seen behind her lodge. She recognized them. She compared them to the paintings on the bells, but to her eye the painting looked dissimilar. The flowers on the bells were rudimentary, almost childlike in their rendering. The reproduction in the book was far more detailed. That seemed to be the only graphic in the book. Bette had said that the Bangor library had more information. She would go there. She would learn more about the artist who had built Trail's End. She sat at her table eating chicken pie and thought about the parallels.

Molly had sought refuge at Trail's End after James died. Nori sought refuge at Trail's End after Marty died. Molly painted miniatures, Nori painted murals.

Still trying to make sense of all this, she rinsed out her teacup and put the potpie container in the trash. It was good and she had been hungry.

She went back to the beginning of the Molly Jones book and began to read more slowly this time, catching every word, until the print began to blur on the page. She blinked several times. It had been a long day and she was tired. If she went to bed this early, however, she'd be up at five. She needed to get up, move around, stretch some feeling back into her legs.

She walked around in her living room, twisting her wedding ring. She sat down on the couch, looked at her fireplace full of cold ashes and played with her ring. She slipped her ring off, then put it on again.

Maybe it was time. She went into her bedroom, feeling disoriented, and found a small wooden box with a rose engraved on the top that Marty had given her once. She took her wedding ring off and placed it carefully inside the box. She put the top back on and put the box on the mantel next to the picture of Marty and her daughters. It was time to finally let go. This was the last thing. She sat down on her couch and looked at her bare hand, the imprint of the ring still there in her flesh after so many years, a white line where she never tanned.

Her eyes blurred. From tears? She felt odd, funny. The fatigue of a few minutes ago had been replaced with nervous energy. She mounted the steps to her loft and found herself standing in front of her humongous empty canvas. She did this every day—came up here and looked at her canvas, hoping for some inspiration. It had never come. Until today. She unscrewed her tubes of paint and in the next moment she was splashing great dollops of paint onto her canvas.

She found herself working in an achingly bright palette, marveling as her brush criss-crossed the canvas. She kept blinking, looking away, trying to focus, but it was getting worse. It was as if she was in some strange and vibrant dream. Her thoughts were slightly off-kilter as she splattered on the paints, this way and that. She kept looking at her bare left hand. At one point she wondered where her ring had gotten to. Then she remembered.

She was aware that she was painting a figure— a man. That much she knew. But that was all she knew. When she painted her murals it was like this. You didn't get the full effect of it until you stood back and looked at the whole.

Colors swirled in front her, the brights seemed much brighter than she remembered, the hues more neon. There were sparkles in her paints. How was it that she had all of these paints with sparkles in them?

A few times she had to stop and try to clear her double vision. But she kept going as the sun set and the moon rose outside of her loft and the world darkened.

It was nausea that eventually stilled her hands. She couldn't think. Was this day or night? How had she gotten up here? What was the matter with her? She placed her paintbrush down on the tray in front of her easel.

Please, God, I don't feel so well. I need help. The prayer came from somewhere deep inside her soul.

She rubbed her eyes and walked stiff-legged to the large loft windows. Instead of seeing beyond, all she could see was a giant handprint, fingers splayed on the glass. She stared at it, trying to make sense of the whorl of the fingers.

She pressed her own hand into the fingers of the hand. They were longer and wider than her own, it was a man's hand most likely. The fourth finger was crooked slightly inward. She kept her hand there, trying to plan what to do next, trying to get her mind cleared enough to think of what to do next.

Was there a bell tinkling somewhere in the distance? No. That was her imagination. *I need sleep,* she thought. *Just sleep.*

Nori put the bells side by side on the kitchen table in front of her. While she ate her breakfast cereal, she wondered about them.

It wasn't Bette. She had called the woman this morning and Bette had said no, she hadn't driven a bell out to Trail's End yesterday and left it on her porch. Last night had been so strange. She had felt weirdly tired yet full of energy at the same time. The last thing she remembered was painting something in her loft. Was it a dream? She hadn't yet been up to check. In truth, she was a little afraid to.

"Nori."

She jumped.

"Sorry," Steve said. "I startled you. I knocked and there was no answer." He was peering past the partially open door.

"I guess I was deep in thought."

"That can be dangerous." He grinned.

She smiled back at him.

He said, "I thought you might like to meet the crew."

He came in. He was wearing worn jeans, shiny in places, and a T-shirt with a lumber company logo on the front. He looked ready for work.

"Sure." She rose.

"I've only managed to round up two workers for today. I'm hoping for a few more tomorrow."

The screen door squeaked as he opened it and in

came two men. First was Chase from the gas station. He seemed nervous and his eyes darted this way and that when Steve introduced them. He wore a gray baseball cap with a sweat-encrusted rim. His hair fuzzed out from underneath at the back.

A little behind him was a chubby young man named Ralph who smiled up at her in a childlike way. This was Bette's son, Steve explained.

"I met your mother yesterday," Nori said.

And while they talked, Chase kept glancing at the bells. Nori could tell that he didn't want her knowing he was looking at them.

She showed the workers around the grounds and explained what she wanted done. They would begin with Cabin 1 today.

Steve gave Ralph a rake and Chase a broom and got them started, while Nori looked on. Steve seemed efficient and knowledgeable. She was thankful for his skills and felt fortunate that he'd been available to work for her.

As they walked, she couldn't help feeling a little anxious. She debated whether or not to tell Steve about the bell and decided against it. It was her problem. It was probably nothing anyway. Probably.

As Steve dug away at years' worth of detritus underneath Cabin 1, he thought about Nori's wedding ring. Or the fact that there was no wedding ring today. He wondered if it meant anything. Maybe not. Maybe it was as simple as she took it off to wash her hands and forgot to put it back on again. He wished he knew more about her. But he really didn't believe that she had anything to do with Scott or Heather.

Heather's disappearance had hit Ralph hard. Heather had been nice to him. She often sat with him in church and always had a kind word.

And now Ralph was standing in front of him, begging to go home.

"Ralph," Steve said, putting a shovelful of garbage onto the back of his truck. "Come with me."

"Can't go back in there. It's about Heather. I can't." His face was red. He was blubbering, holding a hand to his mouth.

Steve put his arm around the shoulders of the young man and led him over behind a large tree. Chase, on the little porch, looked up briefly to see the two of them praying, then went back to his sweeping.

After the prayer, Steve said, "There is nothing here. There is nothing to be afraid of."

Ralph said, "Yes, but, yes, but, what if you pray and it doesn't work?" the young man protested. "What if God doesn't hear you this time? He didn't hear the last time."

"He will," Steve assured him, looking into his frightened face. "And Jesus always hears you."

"But he didn't the last time because Heather's gone."

"He did. And whatever happened to her, God was with her."

"Do you think she's alive?"

Steve looked into that chubby face and said, "Honestly, Ralph. I don't know."

After he got Ralph settled again sweeping the inside of Cabin 1 with a promise that he would be right outside if he was needed, Steve went back to working near the foundation of the cabin.

He didn't know what had happened to Heather and her boyfriend, but one thing he did know and that was Trail's End wasn't demon possessed or cursed or any of the things that people claimed for it. If anything, this place with the birds singing, the insects humming, and the water gently lapping against the shoreline made him feel closer to God.

This was a place that he himself had once thought about buying. Because of the mountains and trees, by four in the afternoon his own rented cabin was in darkness while this place remained in full daylight until late evening.

He waved to Nori as he watched her get into her truck and head to town. She waved back. She'd pulled her hair up into a cute ponytail.

He couldn't quite believe what Alec was suggesting, that Nori was somehow connected to Scott Gramble. No, he had seen the way Nori had lovingly run her finger over the framed photo of her daughters. No one could fake that kind of affection.

Sometime later he heard voices from inside the cabin. "It's mine," Steve heard Ralph abruptly say.

"No. I want it," Chase answered. Steve paused to listen. He could hear Ralph's plaintive call. "It's mine. Give it to me."

"No," Ralph cried.

"Give it to me!" Chase demanded.

"No. I found it. It's mine."

Steve went over to them and saw that they seemed literally in a tug of war on the porch with a small unseen item between them.

"What's going on?" Steve said.

Ralph said, "I found it. It's mine."

"I have to have it," Chase said, raising his voice until it was pitifully high-pitched and whiny.

"Give whatever it is to me." Steve put out his hand like a demanding father to a couple of toddlers. "Now."

Ralph handed the object to Steve. "But I get to keep it," he said. "I found it fair and square. Steve, I found it fair and square. I did."

It was a little plastic change purse, the kind that sold for a buck at dollar stores—cheap, flimsy, grimy with age. A split ring was attached to it for holding keys. He was about to give it to Ralph when he turned it over.

He stared down at it. "Where did you find this?" He kept his voice even.

On the back side of the purse in neon letters was the name *Heather.*

"Under the bed in the cabin," Ralph said, nodding.

"Show me."

They went inside, Chase following.

Steve bent down. "Under here?"

"Stuck under a board. Way back there. Under the window. I saw something shiny. I was the one. It's mine, Steve, it's mine."

Steve pulled his cell phone out of his pocket and photographed the place where Ralph had found the wallet. When Steve rose, he pointedly said to Chase, "What makes you think you should have it?"

"Because I want it."

"Why?"

He shrugged, looked away from Steve and said quietly, "Because I just do." He looked as if he was shaking with anger.

"Why do you want it? 'I just do' isn't an answer."

Chase turned and stomped out of the cabin, his whole body full of rage.

Ralph came closer. "Is this Heather's wallet?"

"I don't know," Steve said. "It might be. It might not. I'm going to be taking it to Alec in any case." He opened his cell phone to make two calls—the first to Alec, and the second to Nori. She needed to know the full story of Trail's End.

FIVE

Nori had never seen Marlene's Café so busy. It was a regular flutter of activity, with Marlene waving her manicured fingers in all directions. The tables weren't being used for customers. All of them were in various stages of decoration making. At one table, a large woman in gray was making tissue flowers, something Nori dimly remembered from her childhood. At another table, Selena and a couple of girls from church were making construction-paper chains. At another, a woman was arranging faux flowers in vases.

"What's going on?" Nori asked. "Someone getting married?"

To which one of the girls with Selena guffawed. "Yeah, right, a wedding? Remind me to make paper chains at my wedding."

"Where is Chase?" Marlene said, wandering from table to table. "He is the only one who can do a half-decent drawing around here."

"He's at my house," Nori said.

"Oh, Nori. Are you going to the Strawberry Party? It's at the church."

"What's a Strawberry Party?"

"Oh, the church sponsors it. It's to raise money, actually." Marlene waved her hands while she talked. "But it's really a community thing. It's a barbecue and food and face painting, all the usual things. So now you know, now you have to come."

"I don't know." Nori knew so few people here that she just wasn't sure she wanted to go to a big party at the church. Besides, she'd never even been inside the church. She told this to Marlene and the woman laughed. "Everyone knows you. And think of it this way. This will be the perfect place for you to get to know them. Selena!" she called. "Bring Blaine and Meredith over. They haven't met Nori yet. Get on over here." She gestured.

Introductions were made all around and Nori had to admit she felt a bit embarrassed as Marlene went on and on about Daphne and Rachel and how they all would be fast friends one day. She wasn't sure this was true. Daphne and Rachel were a bit younger than Selena and Blaine, yet that seemed not to matter to Marlene.

The girls smiled shyly and Blaine seemed quite interested that Nori was actually living out at Trail's End and was full of questions until Selena nudged her and she stopped talking. Nori didn't know quite what that was about, so she directed her next comment to Selena.

"Your chicken pie was tremendous. I just thought you should know. I loved it."

Instead of the normal reaction of smiling and simply saying "thank you," Selena's eyes became wide and she put her hand to her mouth.

A short while later, Nori's cell phone rang. She looked down at the caller ID and saw it was Steve Baylor.

"I need to see you," he said rather abruptly. "I need to talk to you about something. I'm taking Ralph and Chase home."

"Was there an accident?"

"No. Nothing like that. I just need to talk with you about your place."

"It sounds serious," Nori said.

"It might be. I'm meeting with Alec later."

When Steve arrived at Marlene's twenty minutes later and saw how busy it was, he suggested he and Nori go out onto the boardwalk. He held a small paper bag. His eyes were grim, and the set to his mouth was firm. They walked. The only sounds were her sandals flapping on the boardwalk and the thunk of his work boots.

The boardwalk along Whisper Lake ran the length of the town, and through the years many improvements had been made to it. There were beach accesses at various points along the boardwalk plus numerous benches. It was to one of those far benches that Steve headed.

They sat. The little bag was on his lap. He wore mirrored sunglasses and she couldn't see his eyes.

Steve finally began. "I don't know how much you know about the place you bought. . . ."

"Well, I know all about the ghost." She tried to keep her voice light.

Carefully, he took off his glasses, folded them, placed them in his pocket and looked at her.

Nori added, "Bette, Ralph's mother, gave me a book about the ghost when I visited the museum."

"I'm surprised she gave you a book about ghosts. She tries to downplay that legend."

"I wanted information about Trail's End and it was the only book she had. Is this about the ghost?"

"No."

"What then?"

"This is about something that was found in the cabin this morning."

She kept her gaze on him.

He went on. "You know your place was empty for five years. In five years a place like yours gets used for all sorts of things—parties, kids getting together, drugs, drinking."

She took in a sharp breath. Had he found drugs? Could she be liable? The thought frightened her.

He opened the bag and brought out a plastic bag that contained a small pink change purse. The name *Heather* was on one side in sparkly letters.

Heather? Wasn't that the name of Selena's friend who disappeared? But what did this have to do with her?

"Have you heard the name Heather Malloy? She was a girl who disappeared from Whisper Lake Crossing with her boyfriend a little over a year ago."

Nori picked up the plastic bag and looked it

over. She said, "Marlene told me that a girl went missing. I didn't know her name. Is she related to Malloy's Mercantile?"

"Their daughter."

"How sad. But how would this wallet end up at Trail's End?"

"That's why I'm here."

He told her about Heather and Scott and about parties on the grounds of Trail's End and how one of these parties was the last place either of the young people had been seen.

"I'm going to give this to Alec," Steve said, putting the bag back in his pocket. "I know he's going to ask you if he might have permission to conduct a search of your place."

If it would help the police find out what had happened to Heather and her boyfriend that would be okay with her. She would move heaven and earth if one of her daughters was missing. "By all means," she said. "Did you know Heather?"

"Not well. She was just one of the kids in the youth group. She was nice. I remember that. I never met Scott."

He put his mirrored glasses back on, perhaps signaling that the meeting was over. There seemed to be so many dark places in him. Even if she did admit to herself that she was attracted to the man, she wasn't certain that he was the kind of man she would choose—big and broody like that. She looked down at her hands, her fingers splayed on her bare knees. He was looking at her hands, too, she noticed, and she suddenly felt self-conscious about the fact that she was not wearing her ring. She folded her hands tightly between her knees. Had she taken her ring off because of this man? The thought made her face feel hot.

Nori and Steve stood up and began walking back to town. In a quiet voice, he said, "Will your daughters be able to spend time with their father this summer?"

Her gasp was quite audible. She stopped on the boardwalk, practically tripping over her feet. She said, "What?"

He repeated his question.

"I thought you would have known."

"Known what?" The look on his face was all concern as he pulled off his sunglasses to look down into her eyes.

"My husband is dead."

He didn't say anything for quite a while. The news seemed to have taken him by surprise. "I'm sorry, Nori, I didn't know this."

"I thought everyone knew . . ." Nori suddenly realized that Marlene was the only one she'd told. However, she had the impression that Marlene told everybody everything. Maybe she didn't.

Steve repeated, "I didn't know." He seemed at a loss for words.

"It's okay," Nori said. "He was hit by a car eighteen months ago. Jogging."

"I'm so sorry, Nori."

They stood on the boardwalk quite still for a while. It was like they couldn't move on from there. He'd thought she was married! All this time!

Any words he may have said were interrupted by Marlene, who was hurrying toward them on the boardwalk. "You guys. Hey, can I impose? If you're on your way to the Strawberry Party, then would you mind taking Selena and Blaine and Meredith and a bunch of pies?"

They both stared at her.

"Nori, you *should* go to the party and, Steve, you should take her and if you do that it would work out just perfectly for me. Because Roy has the truck in Shawnigan. He promised he would be back in time, but something must've come up and so I need to get these over there. I've been carting stuff over there all day until Roy had to take the truck. Now I'm stuck."

Steve looked at his watch. "I wish I could help, Marlene. I'm meeting Alec."

Marlene looked at Nori, "Well, how about you, Nori? You really should go, you know."

Nori began, "I wasn't really . . . Well, actually I was thinking about heading back to Trail's End and start clearing the beach while it's still light."

"It's a madhouse at the café. I can't trust anyone there to get my cakes and pies over to the church in one piece so when I saw you out here I thought how perfect, you guys can go."

A bit of a shy smile was forming on Steve's face, a welcome change from the grimness of the past few minutes. He turned to Nori. "If you go, I'll meet you there later. I promise I'll come as soon as my meeting's over."

Nori looked from him to Marlene and then back again. "Okay, but what kind of a party is it, again?"

"It's the annual Strawberry Party sponsored by the church and held on the church grounds, but it attracts way more than just church folks on account of the food. Steve will tell you—this church will find any excuse for a social. But this one's actually a moneymaking thing. People donate the money and it's used in Africa. They used to call it a Strawberry Social, but people said that sounded too old-fashioned so they changed it to Strawberry Party. Like I said, this church will use any excuse for a party. There is the Strawberry Party, the Blueberry Potluck, Beans and Scallop Bake-off, numerous pancake breakfasts and suppers all to raise money."

"Okay then," Nori said. "Maybe I'll go."

But Marlene was already on her way back to the café calling as she bustled, "Selena! Blaine! I've got you girls a ride. Meredith! Come on now!"

Steve smiled down at Nori before he left. "She's a mother hen, that woman. I'll see you later. Wait for me."

"I will."

She stood beside her truck and waited. She didn't see the girls, wondered if she was supposed to go back in and look for them. She leaned against her driver's door and waited. What she really wanted to do was go home, but Steve had said he was coming. And she was trying not to admit it to herself, but she was looking forward to seeing him.

A few minutes later, she saw Blaine and Selena at the back door of the café. They appeared to be arguing. Blaine's hands were in motion and she was scowling as she talked rapidly. Selena said nothing, just toed the dirt with her sandal. The other girl, Meredith, stood back, her hand to her mouth.

Her husband was dead. Did that change anything for Steve? It changed everything and it changed nothing. On hearing the news he'd had an odd sort of reaction, one that he couldn't really figure out. When he thought she was married, and therefore unavailable, he had been able to deal with his feelings for her. But now that she was *available*—or at least not married—she felt more unattainable than before. At least for him.

He couldn't deny his attraction to her, yet there was so much in him that still needed working out and working through. He may have given his heart to the Lord two years ago, but that didn't mean he had his life all together. Far from it. If anything, he was in some ways more confused now than when he had kept his emotions under military check. And then there was the whole matter of trust. What if he gave his heart and soul to this woman only to have her leave him later? He didn't know if he could bear that kind of pain again.

He got into his truck and headed to the sheriff's office to meet Alec. In his rearview mirror, he could see Selena and Blaine carrying pies and boxes to Nori's truck.

He met Alec and showed him the wallet, and then the two of them drove together to the Malloys' white Victorian home with the pillars in front. Cliff and Phyllis Malloy were there and waiting, Alec having called them earlier.

"What is it?" Cliff said, opening the door to let them in. "Do you have news of our Heather?" Steve and Alec stood in the wide carpeted entryway, the walls covered with framed pictures of Heather.

Cliff, like many in the town, knew that Steve and Alec were friends and that they sometimes "worked" together. But if anyone wondered why a cabinetmaker sometimes did police work, they didn't ask.

"Is she alive?" Phyllis asked. "Have you found her?"

"We have something we'd like you to look at." Alec held out the wallet.

Phyllis rushed forward. Her movements were

jerky, her eyes red. Steve knew just how much this had taken from the both of them, not knowing what happened to their daughter. Had she run away with Scott and were they alive somewhere? And if so, why hadn't Heather contacted her parents?

Prior to Heather's disappearance, Phyllis Malloy had been a happy woman who ran the mercantile, volunteered and served on the library board. Since her only daughter's disappearance, she had become bitter and isolated. Steve had seen Cliff at church, but Phyllis seldom came anymore.

"What is this?" Phyllis said. She had lost considerable weight since Heather had disappeared, and her cotton shirt hung limply on her frame, like a sweater on a metal coat hanger.

"This was found at Trail's End," Alec said. "Do you recognize it?" He pointed to the name Heather.

Phyllis gasped, took the wallet, looked at it this way and that, and shook her head. "I don't remember Heather having a little purse like this. Is there anything inside?"

Alec shook his head. "We're having it tested, but I'm not sure we'll find anything. This was found underneath some floorboards in the cabin closest to the lodge. Are you sure you don't remember Heather using something like this? Even once?"

Phyllis shook her head. "I'm sure. It's just not

familiar to me. I wish it was. When they were dating, Joe gave her a little jewelry box with her name on it. We kept that. But this is merely a trinket, dollar-store fare." She handed it to her husband.

Cliff's long body was bent, his forehead in his hands. When he looked up at Alec there was venom in his eyes. "You mean this is all you have? Nothing else? You haven't found that murderer Scott yet? We can't believe you haven't found him after all this time. We just want him brought to justice. We've told you his last name. We've given you a description. I don't know what the holdup is."

"Mr. Malloy." Alec's voice was very patient. He'd been down this road before with Cliff Malloy and, by default, so had Steve.

"No," Phyllis said. "Cliff, we know she's alive somewhere. We know it. I refuse to believe she's dead."

Alec said, "We're doing everything we can to follow up on this."

Cliff's voice was abrasive. "Then instead of coming here with itsy-bitsy purses, go find her murderer. He's out there. Even now roaming the woods behind Trail's End and you fellas ain't doing nothing to stop him."

Phyllis put her hand on her husband's arm to still him. To Alec and Steve she said, "Joe was here the other night. He's still finding it hard, poor lad, especially because that Scott boy came out of nowhere. Scott seemed so nice, but that was all a put-on."

Alec nodded. They had been through this, too. It was common knowledge that Heather and Chase's brother, Joe, had dated. Joe had been devastated when Heather had dropped him for a stranger from Bangor. The Malloys had met Scott only once and Cliff's assessment was that he was a "wolf in sheep's clothing." He acted nice and "Christian," but underneath he was no less than a predator.

And was this predator now stalking the woods out behind Trail's End?

SIX

The girls were mostly quiet on the way to the Strawberry Party. Blaine was a tiny girl with short, spiky hair and her friend Meredith was a bigger girl, as tall as Nori, with straight blond hair. Even though Nori tried to engage them in conversation, telling them about her own daughters, she felt she was talking to a wall. Selena, as usual, said nothing to her.

Meredith talked. She asked Nori about where she came from and how she liked Whisper Lake Crossing. Was she all alone out there? Was she scared? At that question, Selena nudged Meredith in the ribs. Meredith promptly shut up and they were quiet for the rest of the trip.

The church grounds were strung with Japanese lanterns and construction paper chains. Tissue flowers adorned the lamp stands and poles. Long picnic tables were already covered with potato salads, cakes and other food items. People kept coming in, bringing more food. It looked as if there would be enough to feed several armies. Nori parked behind the church.

The four of them managed to get the pies and boxed cakes to the appropriate tables, and that's when their togetherness ended. Despite Marlene ordering Selena and the girls to "take Nori around and introduce her to people," the girls took off as soon as the cargo was unloaded. Only Meredith turned back to even thank her for the ride. If Nori didn't know teenaged girls so well, she would have taken it personally.

Barbecues were being set up at one end of the church yard and Nori slowly walked to one of the picnic tables and stood there trying to see if there was anyone she recognized. She saw people from town, but she really knew no one personally around Whisper Lake Crossing except Marlene. And Steve. The only other contacts she had had with people were the many contractors and workers she had tried to hire. She saw some of them now, milling about with their families. More and more people were arriving. Shy by nature, Nori decided she would leave, drive back to Trail's End and call Steve later on his cell phone.

"Nori!"

She turned. It was Bette from the museum.

"Hey." It felt good to finally see someone that she actually knew.

"Nori, it's so nice to see you here. Did you come by yourself?"

Nori nodded. "I dropped a couple of girls here with pies from Marlene's. I'm supposed to be meeting Steve later, but I'm thinking about going home now. For a bit."

The small woman put her hand on Nori's arm. "You don't need to go home. Why don't you come with me and have a glass of very delightful straw-berry punch."

"Strawberry punch?"

"This is the Strawberry Party, my dear. Everything here will be made of strawberries. If they could put strawberries on the hamburgers they would."

Nori chuckled. "The whole town seems to be here."

"It's one of the many socials to raise money for charity. So the food is all donated."

"Wow."

For the next hour Bette pulled Nori around with her and introduced her to people. She met Paul, who proudly told her he had the fastest boat on the lake. Bette told her later that Paul would never "darken the door of the church," but he always came to the socials on the church grounds just as long as he didn't have to go inside. She met Ted Ling from the Chinese restaurant, Maizie, the owner of the T-shirt shop, someone named Lark who was some sort of biologist and lived next to Bette. She met Tom the youth worker, and many others whose names became a blur after a while.

Bette and Nori sat down at one of the long tables with refilled cups of punch. Bette left her for a moment to make sure Ralph was okay at the face painting booth where he was helping out.

She wasn't alone for more than five minutes before Marlene showed up with a pie in each hand.

"Nori!" she called loudly. "Let me drop these off and I'll be right there."

Nori smiled. She wasn't going anywhere. A few moments later, Marlene returned and sat down across from her with a heavy sigh. They were the only ones at this particular table.

A few tables away from where they were sitting, Selena, Blaine, Meredith, Chase, Joe and Connolly had congregated. Their heads were together as if in deep discussion, and if she was not mistaken it looked as if Selena's shoulders were heaving. Was the girl crying? Blaine and Meredith were sitting on either side of her. Meredith's arm was around her, and behind the table Joe stood there scowling.

"Has Selena been showing you around? I told her to keep you under her wing and to show you the ropes, and introduce you to everyone," Meredith said.

"Bette did, actually. I think I've met everyone in town."

Marlene glanced over to where the girls were at the picnic table and shook her head sadly. "Those girls. I apologize for them. They've been through so much."

Nori nodded. "Steve told me they were all out at a party at my place. That was the last place that anyone saw their friend, Heather."

Marlene sighed. "I didn't want to tell you about the Trail's End connection. That's just one theory." She looked around her to make sure they were alone before she went on. "I don't know what to do about Selena. She's our only child. I couldn't have any more after she was born. She used to be such a delight." Marlene stopped as if choked up. "I can't get her to wear anything but black. She changed so much after Heather disappeared. Roy and I are at a loss. We've talked to the pastor. We've looked into counseling. But she absolutely refuses to go. It's been almost two years and she's secretive, cries all the time. We just can't reach her. We wanted her to go to college this year, but she wanted to stay at home and work in the café. It's like she's stuck."

"She sounds in pain." Nori looked up in time to see Joe stalking away. She heard Selena call after him, something that sounded like, "I can't do this anymore, Joe. I just can't."

Marlene looked at Nori, her eyes sad. "Should the kids still be in such a state? Do you think?"

Nori thought about Daphne and Rachel. They missed their father, of course. There wasn't a day that went by that all of them didn't miss him, yet they laughed and had fun. In short, they were getting on with their lives. "Maybe," Nori ventured, "it's because no one really knows what happened to Heather. What do you think happened to her?"

"I never believed Heather and Scott took off and are living together. Heather was such a nice girl. A leader in the youth group. She wouldn't have left with Scott. She even took that . . ." Marlene waved one hand in the air. "That pledge thing about remaining pure until you get married. So that's why I don't think they ran off."

"Did you ever meet her boyfriend?" Nori asked. Selena raised her head and was now wiping her eyes with a napkin. Nori had a clear view of her face.

"Selena met him. She said he was nice," Marlene answered. "But a lot of people don't. The Malloys think he kidnapped her." Marlene shook her head. "We don't know. We just carry on and pray. Roy and I do the best we can."

"I guess that's all you can do."

The aroma of hamburgers wafted toward them.

"Well," said Marlene, hefting her pink bulk. "You want a burger? It's for a good cause."

"Sure. They smell great."

While in line, Nori met more of the locals. She met the senior pastor, Merlin, and his wife, Louise. She met the manager of the local day care and a few others. It was keeping everyone straight that was going to be the challenge. There was a jar on the table where you put in your donation. She got a ten-dollar bill from her wallet and stuffed it in. Then grabbed another ten. It was for a good cause after all.

She had gotten her burger loaded with onions and relish and ketchup when Steve approached her. He wasn't smiling. She said, "Tell me. But get a burger first."

He did so and they walked to the edge of the church grounds with their paper plates and sat on a rock near the church graveyard. The evening breeze seemed to be enough to keep the mosquitoes at bay.

"The Malloys didn't recognize the wallet."

"Oh?"

They sat and he told her about meeting with the Malloys. Nori started to wonder if she would have bought Trail's End had she known the history. She had more questions about Heather and Scott, and Steve answered them as best he could.

The breeze lessened as evening approached and the mosquitoes finally had their way, driving them away from this place. Before she got into her truck, Steve took her hand and held it for a while. "Be careful, Nori. Just be careful."

SEVEN

Be careful of what? Nori wondered. She stood at her window and stared out into the night sky. Fireflies chased each other among the trees down by the lake. She touched her hand at the place where Steve had stroked hers. When he had let go, he had gently slid his hand down hers, caressing it right to the end of her fingers. She still felt the tingle of that.

If she had taken the time to look around a bit, she would have noticed that something was definitely wrong. She hadn't. Instead, she went straight to bed where her dreams were filled with Steve.

In the morning Nori decided to clean up her loft. She couldn't remember much about that evening of painting. When she'd been feeling so sick that night she hadn't given the room a backward glance as she'd headed down the stairs. It might be interesting to see exactly what she had painted.

At the top of the stairs she stood and cocked her head to the side and looked at the huge canvas. When she had left the loft, she hadn't really had a good look at what she was painting. She knew she was painting the ocean. She remembered the waves, but this morning she could see that this was Marty. It was very rudimentary, barely an abstract, but she could tell it was him. She had seated him on an old and faded Cape Cod chair, one that she remembered, one that she had meant to brighten up with paint every summer.

Even though the outlines were faint, she recognized the porch where he sat. It was the seaside summer house that belonged to his family. She had started filling in the waves of the sea beyond him when dizziness and blurred vision had finally stilled her work.

She was surprised to see that even though she had been sick, she had managed to put her paints neatly away. Her paintbrushes were cleaned and lined up the way she always left them. This was the way she always did things, left them organized and well cared for.

She looked up at Marty and felt tears slide down her cheeks. She put a hand to her mouth and stared for several more minutes at her painting before she turned toward the loft windows. She was stunned to see a jagged crack that started from the top right corner and ended down at the bottom left.

She sighed loudly. That was all she needed, a broken window of this size. How much would a new window cost? And more important, how had this happened? That tree branch? Had the wind done this? It had been breezy yesterday, but not windy enough to do this. Ugh! In the center of the window there was a hole.

She went downstairs to fetch a broom. She was

glad Steve was coming today. She'd have to get this window boarded up before it rained again. She had swept up the glass and put it in the garbage when she saw what may have crashed through the window and broken it.

A brass bell lay on her floor about a foot from the window. She had never seen the bell before. She picked it up with trembling fingers. Had someone thrown it in here? This was no passerby leaving an antique bell on the front step for her and forgetting to write a note. She felt a chill run down her spine.

She headed down to her kitchen to call Steve. He said he was already halfway down the driveway with a couple of kids from the youth group, more good, strong bodies to clean up the brush.

"Steve, someone threw a bell through my window," Nori said.

"What?"

"A brass bell through my loft window. The window's broken."

"Are you okay, Nori?"

"I think so. Just scared me a little bit."

"I'll be right there. I'm almost there."

She sat at her kitchen table, looked at the bells she had lined up, and tried to think of a reasonable explanation for all of this. Maybe the bell had been here all along and the wind had broken the window after all. No, she would have seen it before.

The idea that she had slept peacefully, calmly, in her bed, while this window was broken gave her chills. She could not stop shivering despite the warmth of this sunny morning. Because she was remembering other things she should have taken note of—doors left unlocked when she knew she had locked them, windows closed when she knew she had left them open and vice versa. *What was going on? Did this have something to do with the Heather wallet?*

In a few minutes Steve was there. She went outside, down her porch steps and across the flagstone path and ended up in his arms. She didn't care that all the kids looked on at them in this embrace. Steve was here. She was safe now. He held her haltingly and let her go quickly. She said, "This is the third bell."

"Let's have a look." After he got the kids busy with tasks, they went upstairs to the loft, his arm firmly on her back. As they walked, she told him about the other two bells.

"You should have told me."

"I kept thinking it was nothing."

At the door to her loft, instead of looking at the bell, he gazed at Marty. "You did this? You painted this?"

She nodded.

"I didn't know you were this good."

"It's nothing." She felt shy. "It's my husband. It's Marty."

"He looks like a very nice man."

"He was."

Steve went right up to the painting. "It's so good."

"I'm surprised it looks like anything. I got so sick the night I painted it."

There was concern in his eyes. "Sick? You're okay now?"

"I'm fine. It was a onetime thing. I was just overtired."

"You're working too hard." He pointed to the window. "Your window was intact then?"

She nodded. "But I did see a handprint." She pointed. "On the window that's now broken. I wanted to wash the window this morning. That's when I found the bell."

He walked over and picked up the bell where she had placed it on one of the ledges. He ran his fingers over it, examining it carefully. "Do the initials *M.J.* mean anything to you?"

"M.J.? No, why?"

He showed her. The initials M.J. were faintly scratched into the surface of the metal. It didn't look very artistic.

"Marty Edwards is M.E.," she said.

He frowned. "I'm going to call Alec. We'll have someone out here. He should have a look at this. Plus, I want him to look at the other bells."

"You think it's serious? And not just a prank or an accident?"

"I'm not sure."

"Wait a minute," she said. "M.J.—Molly Jones, the ghost who is said to haunt this place."

He glanced at her suddenly. "What?"

"It was in the book that Bette gave me at the museum. I'm going into Bangor today. The library has more books about Molly Jones. I want to know more about her."

"I'll go with you."

This surprised her. "You will? But what about the work here?"

"I think we should suspend work here for the day."

"Another shortened day."

"I think Alec should know about this and I'm concerned about disturbing more evidence. If there is any . . ."

He could see her downcast face.

"Don't worry." He put a hand on her face. "We'll get your place fixed up soon. It'll happen."

She nodded. He was right of course. She said, "You don't need to go to Bangor with me. I'll be okay."

He kept his hand on her cheek and looked down at her for a long minute, so long that she began to feel a heat rise on the back of her neck.

"I need to," he said. "Too many unexplained things are happening here, and I don't want you out of my sight right now."

For a moment she thought he was going to lean down and kiss her.

No kiss came. In fact, he seemed to move away from her slightly, or did she only imagine that? And she was left to wonder, did he want to be with her, or was it the "strange things" happening that was his concern?

EIGHT

Steve convinced her to wait and talk with Alec before heading into Bangor. When he got out to Trail's End, Alec asked Nori more questions. Through it all, she tried to put forth a brave face, yet Steve could see the way she nervously clenched her hands. He suggested that she stay at another place tonight, but she shook her head fiercely and said, "No, this is my home."

The way she said *home* told Steve that this place was anything but home, yet she was trying so desperately to make it so.

While she sat at the kitchen table answering all of Alec's questions, Steve sat and watched her. In truth he couldn't keep his eyes off her. She looked so pretty, the way she kept pulling her hair behind her ears nervously, and saying that she was sure it was an accident, that it was "nothing," that she wished she "hadn't bothered the police," and "that anything could have broken the window. This is an old house. Maybe there was a crack in the window I didn't notice."

Later, after Alec and Steve boarded up her loft window, Nori asked if she could leave now and drive into Bangor. She seemed quite anxious to get there. She laid a hand flat on her mouth as if she would cry.

"Nori." He moved closer to her. Her eyes were filled with tears.

"I need to go to Bangor. I need to find out about the ghost. I don't need a ghost. I don't need a ghost."

"There is no ghost, Nori. That I can assure you. Things like this always have rational explanations."

"I don't know. I just don't know about that."

That sealed it. He would not let her go to Bangor by herself.

He went around and gathered the kids. "Shortened day," he told them. "Someone vandalized the lodge. That's why the sheriff was here. That's why we're heading home now. Nori," he said, "ride with me. We'll go together."

She didn't protest.

On the way into town he worried about her, sitting in the middle, so close that their legs were touching side to side, yet she didn't speak. None of them did. One of the things he planned to do after he dropped off the kids was to convince her that she needed to stay somewhere other than at Trail's End tonight. Something was going on out at Trail's End. He didn't know what it was and it worried him. His old military instincts were kicking in.

On the way into town he heard Blaine whisper to Chase. "It was weird being there, don't you think? Sort of creepy."

"I'm used to it."

"It's hard just to forget about the whole thing."

"We have to, Blaine." His voice was rough, harsh and final.

A long moment passed before she said, "That's pretty impossible under the circumstances."

"We have to!"

It wasn't until after Steve dropped off the teenagers and brought out two coffees that Nori spoke. She seemed a little calmer when she said, "Thank you."

"You're welcome. It's a bit of a trip. I thought we could use the nourishment."

She said, "Something feels wrong."

Those were his thoughts exactly.

She pulled the tab on the coffee lid back and said, "You're not going to like what I have to say."

When she wasn't immediately forthcoming with what she was going to say, he said, "Tell me."

She put her coffee in the cup holder before responding. "I believe this might have something to do with Molly Jones. I mean the ghost of Molly Jones. That's why I want to go to Bangor so much."

"Nori, I told you—"

"Hear me out. Don't think I'm crazy, but I believe Trail's End is haunted and that the ghost of Molly Jones is trying to warn me about something."

"That's ridiculous," Steve growled.

"I knew you would say that. But let me finish.

It's the only thing that makes sense. Even down to the fact that Molly Jones is an artist. I think she may actually have summoned me here. I don't know the purpose yet, but I want to find out."

He turned and looked at her. "Nori, I'm pretty sure ghosts don't exist and haunt places."

"But how do you know for sure?"

He shook his head slowly. "Nori, I don't have all the answers. But can you put on hold the idea of ghosts until I can get back to you with a few answers?"

He passed a car. She didn't answer.

Once he was settled back in his lane, he took a long drink of his coffee and then handed her a new package of red licorice.

She took it, looked up at him and smiled. She was so pretty when she smiled. It was funny how red licorice always had the effect of lightening the mood.

"Have some," he said.

"Thanks." She opened the package and tore off a piece. "Okay. I promise to listen to reason about ghosts. But you can't ignore the obvious," she said.

The Bangor Public Library was a large, gray stone structure that looked more like a church than a library. Steve pulled in behind it. He and Nori went to the information desk and asked for local interest history books.

"Anything in particular you looking for?" the girl with skinny black glasses and the ponytail said.

When Nori told her, the girl directed them to the books on Maine history. They found only one book on Molly Jones, despite Bette's assurances that Bangor would "have plenty."

There was an air of hush in the library and the only sound were her sandals flip-flopping as she walked among the stacks. They took the lone book to the table.

Nori opened it and Steve grabbed a magazine. After a while he looked up from the *Woodworking Magazine* he'd been browsing through and said, "Anything interesting?"

"Not yet. I was hoping to see more of Molly's paintings. She painted in miniature. And I do murals. Don't you think it's interesting that we both paint? Don't you think that's significant?"

"I don't know, Nori."

If he said yes, that it was significant, then he would be agreeing with this wild coincidence that Molly and Nori had a lot in common and that Molly was "calling" to her—whatever that meant. If he said no, then he would be putting down her intelligence and reason. He went back to *Woodworking.*

"Oh, no!" Nori exhaled. She said it so loud that the only other library patron in their section, a balding bespectacled man who was sitting at a

nearby table, took off his glasses and looked over at them.

She slid the book across the table to Steve. "Look at this. This proves what I've been saying. I'm not making this up." She kept her finger on a paragraph.

He read, *"Molly was known for her love of bells. She had a small collection of china bells that she handpainted herself."*

"It doesn't prove anything," Steve said, but even he was becoming less convinced.

On the way out he stopped by the ponytailed girl and thanked her for pointing them in the direction of books about Whisper Lake Crossing.

"Real run on that section lately," the girl said.

"Really?" Steve stopped. "What do you mean?"

She shrugged. "Probably because of summer tourists, people wanting to read up about the local place, you know."

No, he didn't know, but on the way back to Whisper Lake Crossing he wondered if this was important.

NINE

The rain began sometime during the night and Nori ended up sleeping later than she normally did. She woke up slowly and rubbed her eyes. She sat up in bed on this dark morning with the black clouds seeking entrance at her window and reached for her cell phone. She called her best friend, Lisa, who was a television producer for a small local station. She needed Lisa more than ever. Lisa was a Christian with both feet on the ground, a Christian who seemed to have the mysteries of God figured out, or if not figured out, then brought down to a manageable level. Maybe Lisa would have some thoughts about Nori's idea because the whole notion that Molly Jones was somehow "calling to her" was making her crazy. She had told Steve her theory and he had rebuffed her. But what if there was a ghost? Didn't the bells prove it? The bells were the icing on the cake as far as she was concerned.

Still snuggled into her quilt, she told Lisa all about her theory.

"I'm inclined to agree with Steve," her friend said, "but Nori, how horrible about your window. I think Steve is right. You shouldn't be staying there. Why don't you come stay with me?"

"I'll be all right." If there was a ghost here and this ghost needed to contact her, Nori felt that she needed to be here. But this was something she couldn't tell Lisa. Nor Steve. So she said, "I need to stay here because I'm painting again." She told Lisa all about the first painting she had done in eighteen months.

"Oh, Nori, that's wonderful. The lake air must be good for you!"

They talked for a few more minutes about her plans for the place, and Lisa effused over everything. Nori began to feel a bit better.

Nori said, "Lisa, I have a favor to ask. There was a TV documentary about the haunting of Whisper Lake Crossing. And specifically Trail's End. It ran on your station. Do you think you could get me a copy of it?"

"Nori, I wish you wouldn't obsess about ghosts. . . ."

"I'm not obsessing about ghosts. This is just a human-interest story about my place. You think you could find me a copy? I didn't see it when it ran on television and I can't find it on the Web."

An audible sigh. "Okay. I make no guarantees, but I'll see what I can find. I'm small potatoes here, you know." She paused. "Nori?"

"Yes?"

"Please get the ghost ideas out of your mind."

"I'll try."

She glanced at her bedside clock. Rain was spattering against her house and she hoped the board in the upstairs window was keeping the rain out.

"Will Steve be coming today?"

"No, he wants Alec to have a look at the place a bit more."

Lisa said, "Your voice changes when you talk about him. Tell me about him again. He's the one who rescued you from the storm, right?"

"The very one."

"The guy who's, like, six foot six? Looks like a movie star?"

"I never said he look like a movie star."

"Did so. You wrote that in an e-mail."

They both laughed. It felt good to laugh despite the rain and the bells and the possibility of a summoning ghost.

"I did a weird thing the other day," Nori told her. "I took off my wedding ring."

"You what?"

"I know. I said I never was going to do that. I don't know why I did it. I just did."

"I think that's a good thing, Nori."

After they chatted a few more minutes, they said goodbye and promised to visit each other soon. Nori went over to her fireplace, picked up the little box and opened it.

Her ring was gone.

She closed the box and took a deep breath. When she opened the box again the ring would be there, she thought. Except it wasn't.

She sat on the couch with the box in her lap and took another deep breath. *Okay,* she told herself.

There are three possibilities. One, I didn't really put it in the box, I only thought I did. That was a real possibility, because her brain had been all fluttery that night. Maybe she only thought she had put it in the box. *Two, somebody stole it or, three, Molly Jones moved it.*

She went over to her window and looked out at the dark rain and began to be afraid. *God,* she prayed, *help me figure out what's going on.*

TEN

On this very rainy morning, Steve waited for Bette in Marlene's Café. He needed advice. He wanted information on ghost theology and knew that Bette would be able to help him.

He was sitting in a far booth at Marlene's pretending to read the menu, but he was really thinking about Nori. Unfortunately, Pete and Peach had also chosen that morning to hold court at Marlene's. Everyone in the Crossing seemed to know that the sheriff had been out at Trail's End.

"Them evil spirits are digging up trouble," Peach was saying. Pete and Peach had come over and were standing beside him.

Steve put down his menu and glared at them. Peach didn't budge. "It's the curse," he said.

"Everyone who is connected with Trail's End dies or goes insane," Pete added. "You did know that, didn't you?"

Insane? This was a new one.

"They end up in insane asylums, they do," Peach said.

"All of them," he added, which made it seem as if entire wings of hospital psychiatric units were devoted to people who had lived out at Trail's End.

"Peach, Pete," Steve said sternly. "Go away."

"You waiting on your lady friend?"

"Go sit down. And no more talk about ghosts. It's gone far enough," Steve said.

"Not all of us—"

"Go."

They finally did, and Steve looked outside at the rain that slashed against the window. It was a north Maine rain which could go right through a person and settle in their bones.

He glanced at the clock on the wall. Bette was late, which was unlike her. He drank more coffee and his thoughts as usual veered toward Nori. He couldn't deny his growing attraction to this woman. He worried about her, wondered about her. He also wondered about himself. Was he the sort of person who could really love someone? It wasn't the long hours on the job that had killed his marriage to Julie. Nor had it been the secrecy. It was something else entirely. It was the damage to his soul done by his years of military service. He couldn't point to one event that had wrecked him. Instead, it was the accumulation of many. He had killed people. He had seen things. He had tried to wall it all up, but in doing so, he had cemented his very being into that wall until he felt nothing.

He had been to counseling. He was trying with God's help to put it all behind him, but he didn't know whether he was ready to allow himself to feel the sort of feelings he had for Nori.

A few minutes later, Bette blew in, as if brought

in by the rain. She closed her umbrella, ran her hand through her short, gray hair and slid into the booth across from him. Selena came over with more coffee for Steve and a pot of Earl Grey tea for Bette, and took their orders. After Selena had gone back to the kitchen to deliver the orders it looked to Steve as if she was trying to listen to their conversation. He glanced at her pointedly. Hastily, she moved on to another table.

"So Steve," Bette said. "What's on your mind?"

"As you know I'm doing some work out at Trail's End and I'm worried about Nori. I'm worried about what's really going on out there. She believes there's a ghost at Trail's End. You gave her a book about that, I believe."

"Oh, that book. I never expected her to take it seriously. It happened to be the only book I had on the subject." She looked at him thoughtfully for a few minutes before she asked, "What exactly *is* going on out there, Steve?"

He quietly told her about the bells, about the broken window and the other occurrences Nori had told him about.

Bette made a noise that sounded like a grunt of dismissal. "Sounds like plain vandalism to me."

Selena brought Steve's Big Country Breakfast, which consisted of three eggs, steak, hash browns and toast, and a muffin and marmalade for Bette.

"That's what Alec said." He spread maple syrup upon his toast. "But Nori is convinced that this so-called ghost of Molly Jones is trying to contact her."

Bette looked down into her tea and shook her head sadly. "I am so sorry about giving her the book. I should never have mentioned the ghost, but she came in looking for information. It was the only book I had. I never would have given it to her if I had realized how emotionally fragile she was."

Steve picked up on that right away. "You think she's emotionally fragile?"

Bette looked him square in the eye. "I'm not sure. But she's here alone. Her daughters are elsewhere and I don't know where her husband—"

"She's a widow."

"I didn't know that," she said.

"I didn't know it, either, but knowing it now, I'm trying hard to help her."

She reached across and touched his arm. "And it's more than that, isn't it? You're quite fond of her, aren't you?"

He shrugged. Bette knew him so well.

"Bette, can you tell me what you think about ghosts? Nori asked me and I really didn't have a good answer."

She spread a generous dollop of marmalade onto her muffin. "My opinion is that the vast majority of ghost sightings are simply figments of imagination, bad dreams, or too much pepperoni pizza the night before. Then factor in plain ordinary old forgetfulness, people forgetting that they left the window open, or where they put their keys, or that they moved Grandma's rocking chair from one corner to the other. Also, these old houses creak on their foundations, and some of that can sound just like footsteps in the basement."

"But," Steve said, picking up a forkful of eggs, "in Nori's case there *is* actual stuff happening—the broken window, for example, and the bells appearing out of nowhere."

Bette raised her hand. "I was getting to that. Has anyone thought that a real person could be doing this? It sounds to me like she's being terrorized."

Steve frowned. "That's what I think, too. I tried to convince her she should leave Trail's End for a few nights. But she doesn't want to do that. All the way back from Bangor I tried to talk her into it." He remembered that trip, and her final statement as he dropped her at Trail's End: *"My mind is made up, Steve."*

"She would be most welcome at Flower Cottage. I could get a room in the main house ready."

He smiled. "Thank you, Bette. But what should I say to her?"

"The Bible doesn't give a lot of information about ghosts, but what it does say is that Christians need to stay away from ghosts, mediums, all that sort of thing. Jesus cast evil spirits out of numerous people, that we know. But I don't think that the spirits of deceased people roam the earth for hundreds of years like Molly Jones is said to do. That's just not supported by Scripture.

"I should talk to Nori, apologize for even putting the thought of ghosts into her mind. I bear that blame. But I also know what it's like to be alone here. She seemed like such a lost puppy dog at the Strawberry Party. She needs friends. She needs strong Christian friends who will warn her away from dwelling on ghosts."

Steve spent the rest of the afternoon in his shop working on the rocking chair and wondering what, if anything, he should be doing about Nori. He called Alec a few times and his friend said he was working on it, but couldn't find anything about bells connected with Heather and Scott. There were also no prints. They were currently looking at a few gift stores in Shawnigan that sold bells.

Later that afternoon he decided he would visit Nori. He called Selena and ordered two potpies to go plus all the trimmings, which included buns and salad. He would pick them up later and take them out to Nori's. "Two meals?" Selena asked.

Steve said, "One is for Ms. Edwards."

He parked his truck out back and whistled when he went to pick up the takeout from Marlene's. On the way out he stopped midtune when he heard voices. There was no mistaking the high-pitched voice that belonged to Chase.

"No. No," the boy was whining.

"You do as I say," Chase's brother, Joe, said. "This is the way it is now." His voice was low, guttural.

Steve didn't move forward. This might prove interesting. Chase and Joe were standing beside Joe's car. Chase looked skinny and small and miserable and wet. Steve had never seen him so red in the face, so haggard. He looked like an old man, Steve thought. Not past twenty and there were bags under his eyes. Joe had changed, too. There was an intense ferociousness about him. Steve couldn't remember the last time that young man had smiled. Chase said, "Don't you think this is all going to come out now? Everything? I can't do this anymore."

"You will do it. She will do it. We need to do this together. You know that as much as I do." Joe unlocked his car and said, "What I can't understand is why you just didn't just keep the wallet in the first place?"

"Because Ralph saw it. I *told* you." Chase moved away from his older brother.

"I'm just saying you didn't need to go waving it around in Ralph's face."

"I *didn't*. He was the one who *found* it." He expanded the word *found* into about three syllables.

Steve had had enough. He stepped out of the shadows and asked, "What about the wallet? What can you tell me about the wallet?"

The boys stared at him. He seemed to be the last person they expected to see emerging from the rainy shadows. They said nothing.

Of course they would say nothing. Like all of the other times when they'd been questioned, they would say nothing. It was as if there was some sort of pact between them. Steve would get nothing out of them now. He knew that. But he had to try.

Rain dripped on his head and splashed onto his shoulders. He approached them, scowling. He knew his size could intimidate people, and there were times he used this asset to its fullest. In his anger, he grabbed Joe's shirt collar. "What is going on?" he asked.

"Leave me alone," Joe said, shrugging out of Steve's grasp.

"Not until you tell me what's going on. What do you know about the wallet?"

"Nothing," Joe said. There was fire in his eyes.

He turned to Chase. "Why did you want that wallet? What was so important about that wallet?"

Rain splashed off Chase's nose. "I thought Joe would want it." He looked tentatively up to his older brother.

"Why?" asked Steve.

"Because Joe used to be with Heather. Before Scott came along. Joe gave it to her. . . ."

Steve wasn't sure he believed that, and was about to say something when Joe yelled out,

"Scott killed her!" He turned both hands into fists. "And I will kill him when I find him. He can't get away with this. He killed her. You know it. We all know it. He's out there living in the woods and when I find him I'm going to smash his skull in. He's crazy!"

"We don't know that, Joe," Steve said.

"I do."

From long military work, Steve sensed something in the two brothers—raw fear. These were boys who were afraid.

ELEVEN

In the early evening there was a tentative knock at her door. Nori had spent the day in the storage room cleaning and unpacking. That was her excuse, but what she was really doing was looking for more bells. She didn't find any. She went to the door and hesitated before she opened it, wishing she had one of those peepholes.

"Nori? It's me, Steve."

She let out the breath she hadn't realized she'd been holding. He stood on the porch, water dripping off his bushman's hat and holding a bag. The rain had intensified.

"I thought you might be hungry. I got these from Marlene's. Supper. I thought you might like something to eat."

"Well. Thanks. That's nice of you."

He held out the bag. "If you've already eaten tonight, you could put these in the fridge for tomorrow. They're just as good the next day. It's two meals. Potpies. One chicken, one beef."

It smelled good. "Why don't you stay and join me?"

"Really?"

She eyed him and grinned. "You can't truly believe that I would thank you for showing up with two suppers and then not invite you to stay. We can talk about plans for the kitchen. I've been inside cleaning all day."

"Good, because I just happen to have my photo albums in my truck."

She eyed him, smiling. "Now, what would you have done if I'd simply thanked you for the pies and sent you on your merry way?"

"I would have gone," he said, looking forlorn.

"Come in," she said, opening the door wide.

"I also want to talk to you about something else."

"What?" She eyed him as she got out plates and cutlery.

"Nori—" he came toward her "—I wish you would reconsider and move into town. I was just talking with Bette. She said you could stay at Flower Cottage."

"Did Alec tell you anything about the bells?"

"Please, don't change the subject."

She looked at him. "There is no subject. I want to stay here. This is my place and I really mean to stay here."

She knew she was being stubborn. What was she trying to prove to herself? That she was strong? That she wasn't afraid here? The truth was that she *was* afraid here. She was terrified. She had looked all day for her wedding ring and hadn't been able to find it. She'd gone over the scenario a million times in her mind—sitting on the couch and taking the jewelry box with the rose on top downstairs and slipping off her ring and placing it inside and then putting it on the mantel next to

Marty's picture. She had even combed through the ashes in the fireplace.

He took the food out of the bag and set it on the table. They sat down across from each other. She broke the crust of the potpie with her fork. She looked up.

"Steve, would you please say grace? I haven't in almost two years."

"Yes, I would indeed."

They bowed their heads and he thanked God for food and for their friendship.

Nori closed her eyes. It had been a long time since she had prayed before a meal. She usually did when the girls were home. But when they were not, she was just as likely to dig in. She didn't want to admit it, but Steve's prayer stirred something deep inside her. It reminded her of her childhood home, where her father always said grace before meals. Later when she married Marty, he was the one who prayed before they ate. He always thanked God for the food and for home. Those were his words. It was odd that he would use that word—*home*—because when he died she had lost all sense of home. It felt as if she had been wandering ever since. Before Steve said the final amen, she wiped away a single tear.

"Thank you for praying," Nori said.

"You're welcome."

"I haven't prayed in a long time. About anything. After my husband died I guess I was so mad at God I decided I would never speak to Him again."

He paused before he said, "I know what it's like to lose someone."

She stirred her pie a little. Her thoughts tumbled around her; her ring, the bells, this place and now this wonderful man sitting across from her in her kitchen.

While they ate, he told her about his wife. Her name was Julie. When she'd taken Jeffrey to Florida, his world had ended. He hadn't hated God because he hadn't believed in God then, so there had been no one to hate but himself.

"I'm so sorry to hear that," Nori said, cutting a piece of chicken with her fork.

Steve said, "It's what brought me to God. I basically moved here to start over and then God found me. I think He'd been looking for me all along. It finally took me getting to the lowest point of my life for Him to finally find me, for Him to bring me home."

Nori thought about that. She had moved here, not to escape God as much as to find Him and forge a new home out of the wreckage of her life. She wanted a new place for her and her girls.

Outside, wind blew the rain like pebbles against the window. The room was suddenly lit by a brilliant flash of lightning. The deafening thunderclap was almost instantaneous and the lights went out.

Even Steve jumped. Nori realized she was standing and her chair was on the floor behind her.

"What was that?" she yelped.

"No power," Steve said.

As other flashes lit the room, Nori said, "Let me get some candles."

She found some. They lit them and then listened to the storm for a while. It was comfortable being with Steve. When they were settled at the kitchen table, he said, "The candles are nice, Nori. It's very homey."

She smiled at him. "I wish it was," she said. "No matter what I do, no matter how many candles I light up, I can't transform this place into my home. I feel so much like I'm drifting. I want something solid to hang on to."

"None of us are home, Nori," he said. "Everybody feels that way. It's as if we're all stranded. We're like travelers wanting to get somewhere and then bad weather hits and we get stuck in a place we don't want to be. Like we're in an airport and it's Christmas and all we want to do is get home. But the planes never leave and we have to stay in that weird airport place for a long time. We end up living there, and nothing feels like home after that and we're lost."

"Stranded, that's just how I feel." She paused. "How was it for you when you moved here?"

He told her it was okay. He'd made friends and enjoyed what he did. "In many ways this place changed my life. It's still not perfect. I had to go through a lot."

They talked for a long time after that. She found she wasn't as hungry as she thought she was, and barely ate half of her pie. She put the rest in the fridge for later. She told him she was worried about her daughters. "I'm going to be uprooting them, making them move here. I told them it was going to be this wonderful place. And it's not. It's filled with ghosts. Maybe the lights are off because of the ghosts."

"I talked with Bette about ghosts," he said.

"What did she say?"

"She doesn't discount things in the spirit world, but she's highly suspicious that evil spirits are haunting this place. She also cautioned me about ghosts, that Christians should stay away from studying things like ghosts and mediums."

"But how can I stay away from ghosts when I *have* one?"

"I don't think you have one," Steve said.

She turned to him abruptly. "But you don't understand. I have to believe there's a ghost. If it's not a ghost, then it's something more sinister, like a real person stalking me . . . or I'm losing my mind."

She felt like crying, but held back her tears.

After a few moments she said, "How about we go into the living room and have a look at your cupboard designs? We can bring the candles in."

"And I can light a fire."

"Good idea. But there won't be any coffee."

"I'll live."

He lit a fire and she bent down beside him and remembered the first time he had done this. She mentioned it to him.

Steve turned to her, raised one eyebrow, and said, "And my life hasn't been the same since."

She wanted to ask him what he meant by that. There was no doubt in her mind. She was falling for this man.

He went and got a large photo album from his backpack and sat down next to her on the couch and laid the book on their laps. They began to leaf through it. His work was so beautiful. She was surprised. She told him so.

He seemed embarrassed by her praise. "It's just something I do," he said. "If you like, I could get started tomorrow, rain or shine. There've been enough delays."

"That, I agree with."

"My supplier called. The wood we ordered is in. Now we just have to pick a design."

Was it her imagination, or were they moving even closer together on the couch? Their knees touched. And why did he say *we* rather than *you?*

She went through several more pages. The lights flickered back on, but neither of them made a move to extinguish the candles.

He turned to look at her. His eyes were so blue and he was so close to her. "I have another question."

"Okay."

"I was wondering if you'd consent to having dinner with me sometime."

She laughed a little and felt her face go hot. "Isn't that what we just had?"

"No, no, no." He paused. "I'm saying it wrong. I meant, go out to a nice restaurant. Bangor maybe? Or to Camden? Have you been down there?"

She eyed him. He was asking her out on a date and she was not freaking out. "You mean someplace other than Marlene's?"

"I most definitely do mean someplace other than Marlene's."

She felt almost giddy. And then she was feeling something else, something all too familiar these days—the dizziness, the blurred vision. It was coming on quickly. *Not now, not now.*

"Maybe." She looked up at him shyly. "Maybe that would be very nice."

"How about early next week? Monday? Tuesday? Wednesday? Places are not too busy then."

"Monday would be fine."

He looked down at her. "Monday it is, then."

She yawned, put a hand to her mouth to try to stifle it. She was suddenly overwhelmed with a bout of fatigue. Plus, her stomach was getting a bit rumbly.

"You're tired," he said.

"Exhausted," she countered. She closed her eyes, then reopened them briefly, but her vision hadn't entirely cleared. Maybe all the lifting in the storage room had gotten to her.

"I should go." He made to get up.

She didn't want him to leave. She said, "I was going to suggest you stay for a while and we could watch a video or something. I could even make popcorn, but right now I don't know. I feel a little tired."

"You were?"

"I was what? Tired?"

"No. You were going to suggest I stay for a movie?"

She nodded and managed a smile.

By the time he left, the stresses of the day hit her square on. She was tired and dizzy. She put a hand to her stomach. Something weirdly awful was definitely going on inside her stomach. Yuck.

She put the few dishes into the sink to let them soak. This queasiness was not going to allow her to do them tonight. They'd wait until morning. Maybe soon she'd have a dishwasher installed.

A bout of nausea had her running into the bathroom. And that's how it was for the next couple of hours, running to the bathroom, throwing up, then lying down on her bed until the dizziness caught up with her again.

Flu, she said. As soon as this intestinal bug had run its course she'd be fine. Her immune system was down with all these changes in her life. That was all. She finally fell onto her bed and slept.

She awoke some hours later to a horrible taste in her mouth and the sound of a soft banging out in the kitchen. She turned over and reached for her blanket. It wasn't there. She groaned, switched on the bedside lamp to discover she had fallen asleep on top of her bed in her clothes. How had she done that, passed out so completely that she hadn't even changed into her nightgown?

There was that sound again. She got out of bed and stood up for several seconds before she moved. Yes. She felt decidedly better. She put a hand to her tummy. She felt a little weak on her feet, but whatever it was it was gone. She'd be okay.

The window over her sink was rattling as wind made its way through. One of the pull cords on the blinds was banging against the sill. She shut the window tight and latched it until it locked. But hadn't she done this before she went to bed? Trouble was, she couldn't remember much of what happened after Steve left. Should she call someone? Steve? But it was the middle of the night. Was it the *ghost?* Should she call 911?

She realized how stupid that would sound. "I'm calling nine-one-one because my window is open." No, it must be her own stupidity that had not latched it tightly enough. This was an old house. But she couldn't dismiss the growing unease that was making its way up her spine. Maybe she should have listened to Steve and moved into Flower Cottage. She walked through her lodge and checked every window and every door. All were tightly locked.

Next on her list was the bathroom. She washed her face, brushed her teeth, brushed them again and changed into her soft nightgown. She felt much better, almost civilized. She was about to climb back under the covers when she saw a flash of something around the edges of her curtain.

She went and sat beside her window in the dark. It looked as if a figure all in white was moving across her lawn in the rain. Lightning? A trick of the moon and the clouds? But it was definitely a figure.

Her heart pounded. She watched as the figure moved out over the lake and disappeared.

She stayed beside her window for a long, long time.

Had she just seen the ghost of Molly Jones?

TWELVE

There was no sign of Nori when Steve and crew arrived at Trail's End the following morning. With him were Chase, Ralph, Connolly, Blaine, Meredith and his dog, Chester. Chase drove in his father's car and brought Connolly, Blaine and Meredith. He'd talked to Alec about the conversations he'd overhead and they both decided that Steve's best strategy was to keep Chase under his wing. Maybe the boy would let something slip and Steve would find out what, if anything, he knew about Heather and Scott. Alec had said that it would be okay to continue the work at Trail's End.

Steve brought Ralph in his truck. Nori didn't seem to be around, so he got the kids all settled with chores without her.

Usually, by this time of day, her windows were open and there would be the welcoming aroma of fresh coffee. But the window blinds and all of the curtains in the house were drawn and closed.

"You have any idea where she is?" He had brought Chester along for more than just company. He had worked with dogs in the military and had done a little training with his own dog. If there was anything out there, maybe Chester could nose him—or whatever it was—out there. Joe had seemed so sure Scott was a mad killer roaming the woods. Maybe it wasn't Scott. But someone else?

Steve looked at the lake and wondered if Nori had gone out on her kayak on so fine a morning. He checked. Her boat was underneath her porch.

The only other option was that she was out for a walk. He and Chester walked around the property, past all the cabins, and he looked down some of the many hiking trails that began at the end of the gravel road behind the lodge. He didn't see her, but that didn't mean that in a few minutes he wouldn't. She would come breezily up the path toward the lodge, her hair pulled casually back into a ponytail, a smile on her face.

There were lots of trails on her property and he should know. He'd been down most of them. When he and Alec had hiked the surrounding properties to look for any sign of Heather Malloy and Scott Gramble, they had found nothing.

The lodge windows were still tightly closed when he got back, and there was still no answer to his knock. He tried her cell phone again. It rang and rang.

"You seen Nori?" he asked Ralph, who was carrying an armload of dead branches around the back of lodge.

Ralph shook his head. "Nobody has yet, Steve. Nobody."

Last night they had had such a fine and tender conversation. He had told her things he hadn't told a lot of people. Of course, he hadn't shared everything. Nori still didn't know anything about what he had done before he came here. Yet toward the end of the evening something had begun to seem wrong. Maybe it was fatigue, like she said. Maybe it was overwork, but her eyes didn't seem right. When she had walked him to the door she almost seemed—he didn't want to say it—tipsy. On drugs, maybe. She had told him that after Marty died, the only way she could get to sleep was with prescription sleeping pills. Was she overusing them even now?

Yet they had consumed no alcohol, not even a glass of wine. He had seen no alcohol in any of her cupboards. He hated to admit it, but last night when he had excused himself and gone into her bathroom, he had looked through all of her cupboards. Aside from half a jar of ibuprofen, and a bottle of cough syrup, there was nothing. No prescription drugs that he could see. He knew, however, that his search was by no means thorough. Many people kept their prescription drugs beside their bed.

God, he prayed, *why is my life becoming so entangled with such a troubled woman?*

And why was he so suspicious? And where was she now? He knocked on the kitchen window. No answer. He called her name loudly. Nothing.

Chase was at the bottom of the steps and looked up at him. "Maybe she's out in one of the cabins," he said.

"Why don't you have a look?" Steve tried to

keep his voice upbeat, even though he choked back real worry.

He went down the porch steps and made his way over to Cabin 1. He went inside the cabin and stood looking at his tools and frowned. His rakes, shovels, picks and hoes were all upside down. It was the oddest thing. He always left his implements with the business end down—less chance of them falling over that way. And here they were, all lined up in the precise order he had left them, with the bottom side up.

Beside him, Chester whimpered. Who had come in here and done this?

When Nori finally woke up she felt a hundred percent better. She threw handfuls of cold water on her face to make sure she was really well. Had she seen a ghost or had that been a dream? She prayed as she dried off her face. *If I am wrong about this whole ghost thing, please show me.*

She wrapped herself in a fuzzy housecoat and decided to go back up to her loft to look for her ring. It was a wild guess, but maybe her ring was up there? It was about the only place she hadn't looked.

Her horrid night of sickness, or whatever it was, was over. Maybe Selena's pies didn't agree with her. Maybe she was allergic to something Selena put in them. She wondered about MSG.

That spice triggered an allergic reaction in some

people. But she doubted whether Marlene even used that particular ingredient as so many people were sensitive to it. Well, whatever it was, she was over it now. In two days she would be going out on a bona fide date with Steve Baylor. She hummed a little tune as she bounded up the steps two at a time to her loft.

When Nori got to the top and stood in the doorway, all she could do was stare. She leaned against the doorjamb, put a hand to her mouth and gaped some more. She slid down the wall and onto the floor. "Oh, oh, oh." She groaned while outside the birds sang.

The picture of Marty had been crisscrossed with thick, black lines. Across his head in red were the words, "M.J. SAYS LEAVE THIS PLACE!"

She hugged her knees to her chest, rocked back and forth. A fat, black line bisected the neck of her husband, giving the impression that he had been beheaded. M.J. Had Molly Jones done this? She thought about the smooth-faced woman on the cover of the book. That woman didn't look capable of something like this.

"Marty!" she called out. "Who did this to you?"

And as she called out loud to her dead husband, her voice sounded hollow to her own ears. She realized she hadn't "talked" to him in many days.

She needed air. She needed Steve. No, it was too early to phone Steve. He wouldn't be here for several hours.

She heard a noise outside like voices. Whoever had done this was still on the grounds! She crept to the unboarded loft window and looked out. Steve's truck! Impossible. It was way too early. She ran down the stairs to her bedroom and checked her clock. Four a.m., but the lights were flashing. She remembered. The power had been off. She finally found her watch and was horrified to discover it was after nine. How could she have slept so soundly and for so long? She changed into jeans and a T-shirt and ran a fast comb through her hair. She raced outside. "Steve," she called wildly. "Steve."

He grinned broadly when he saw her approach. "Hey, I've been looking for you! I was just about ready to organize a search party." When Chester saw her, he ran over. "I have a truckload of wood," Steve said. "It came. For the kitchen." Then he stopped and seemed to see her face. "Nori?"

She knew her face betrayed her awful fear. She pressed trembling fingers to her mouth.

"Something happened," she finally managed. "Something really bad."

He touched her shivering arm.

She said, "Come with me. It's inside. Up . . . in . . . my loft."

The two of them mounted the loft steps.

When Steve saw the wrecked painting, his eyes screwed up and he didn't say anything for a while, just kept his arm around her.

"M.J. again," Nori said. "Molly Jones. The ghost?"

Steve turned to her. "Molly Jones doesn't want you to leave, but someone else sure does."

He walked over to the painting, examined it, then pulled out his cell phone and took several pictures. He made a call and spoke in half sentences while Nori trembled and wiped at her teary eyes.

He took several more pictures from different angles before they left the room. "The police will be here shortly. Let's not touch anything. Let's leave, go downstairs."

"Yes."

She was glad to get out of that place. They went downstairs and stood together on the porch while they waited for Alec. She seemed barely able to stand and leaned her back against the banister.

She spoke. "And I saw her . . . I think I saw her last night. Or I saw something that looked like a ghost. I wasn't feeling well during the night and my mind could have been playing tricks on me. It looked like a ghost. I was at my bedroom window and it looked like it was floating out over the lake." Nori was breathless, could hardly get her words out.

"You saw a light out on the lake?"

"Yes."

He rose. "Let's go have a look. Show me which is your bedroom window." They walked around the outside of the lodge.

She pointed it out.

He went to it and wiped his finger on the window ledge. He spent a lot of time looking up in the trees and underneath the windows. "We'll get the police out here, too."

"Why?"

He pointed straight up at a piece of what look like reflective metal attached to a tree branch. "What's that?" he asked.

"I have no idea. I always figured it was some sort of bird feeder."

"That could be your ghost. A flashlight shining on that might cast a shadow on the lake. Last night was a clear night. The rain had stopped and the trees would be glistening. It would've been a perfect night to create a ghost." He put quotation marks in the air around the word *create*.

She looked at him. "Create a ghost?" But if it wasn't a real ghost then a real person was after her. "Steve," she said. "I don't want to stay here tonight."

"Good."

THIRTEEN

Steve sat beside Nori until the police arrived. Along with Alec was a young man from the Shawnigan squad named Peter. The four of them went up to the loft and examined the painting.

Alec was tall by anyone's standards, yet not as big as Steve. He had a thin face, brown eyes and dark hair and wore wire-rimmed glasses that looked slightly crooked on his nose. He jotted notes onto a little pad while he talked. He went over to the painting and touched it with the end of his finger. "It looks like permanent marker and not paint." He turned to Nori. "Have your paints been disturbed?"

She shook her head. "I don't think so. They seem to be the way I left them."

He asked her if they could do a thorough search of her grounds and she said that would be fine. He paused. "Did you know this Scott Gramble, Mrs. Edwards?" He let the question hang in the air while she simply stared at him.

Steve kept his arm around her and squeezed her a bit tighter. She was flabbergasted. "How would I know who that is?"

"It's a question we have to ask."

The young officer took pictures of the painting and Alec said that a crew would be coming later to fingerprint the place.

She told him about seeing the light out on the lake and they went around to look at the tree. She called it a light rather than "the ghost." Alec and Peter whispered among themselves, words she couldn't hear. She wrapped her arms around herself and shivered. Off to the side Chase was staring at them. Blaine and Meredith were talking behind their hands and Ralph stood at the back muttering to himself, his face red. She told her story again, adding this time that she'd been sick.

When she said she'd had some double vision, the police seemed to exchange knowing glances. What was this? Did they think she was crazy? Alec asked her all sorts of questions about herself, about her daughters, and even about Marty. She went through it all, wondering what her daughters had to do with any of this. She told them about the bells and even about her wedding ring going missing. She took them back inside and she handed the wooden box to Alec.

"I put my ring in the box and when I went to look yesterday, it was gone."

Alec opened the box. And there it was, nicely nestled in the cotton. The ring was there.

She had to sit down or she would faint. She stammered, "It wasn't there before. I'm sure of it. I looked all over. I looked everywhere. It wasn't in the box. I'm not lying." She was shaking her head over and over. Suddenly, she was trembling and she couldn't stop. What was going on? *Dear God, what is going on here?*

Whatever brave front Nori put on for him and everyone else, whatever thoughts she espoused about Trail's End being her "home" and not wanting to leave it, Steve knew she was afraid. And who wouldn't be? A painting defaced, a window broken, mysterious bells appearing out of the blue, doors unlocked, rings disappearing then appearing again. It was too much for anyone to have to go through.

This brave and plucky woman was driving her truck right behind him, following him to Flower Cottage. Bette was, even now, making up a room in the main house for her. Bette had five cottages, but Steve was just as happy having Nori in the main building, where his friend Bette could keep an eye on her.

He, like Alec, was at a loss. Alec kept grilling Nori about her past. He kept asking whether she was sure the ring wasn't there the last time she looked.

"Of course I'm sure," Nori kept on saying. "I'm sorry. I know what I saw and didn't see."

Alec had done a full check on Nori and had found nothing—not so much as a parking ticket.

"But," Alec had said, "as you know, Steve, sometimes police checks miss things."

What was he suggesting? That Nori had somehow done this to herself? For what purpose?

When he had growled that question at his friend, Alec hadn't had an answer.

No, Nori was who she said she was—a widow who had come here to begin a new life and make a new home and wound up getting involved in something she had nothing to do with and knew nothing about.

Beside him, Ralph was talking. "Is it about Heather? Did you find something about Heather? Is Heather there?" he kept asking. "Is Heather at the cabin? Is Heather at Trail's End? Is that why Alec came?"

Steve just shrugged, lost in his own thoughts. Even Chester sat on the backseat with his head down between his paws, sensing the seriousness of the situation.

Ralph went on, "Joe was mad. Joe was really mad. You should see how mad Joe was. And Chase, too. Mad."

Steve nodded. He'd heard all this before, how mad Joe was when Heather dropped him.

"Mad," he kept saying. "Mad. Mad."

He caught a glimpse of Nori in his rearview mirror. One hand was on her wheel and the other rested on the open car window, but at least she was no longer talking on her cell phone. Good girl. The sooner he could get her safely installed with Bette, the sooner he could get back to Trail's End and look over the place with Alec and find out who was threatening Nori.

Ahead of him, Chase was rounding the bend in the gravel road with the other workers. They had all left Trail's End at the same time.

"Joe was mad. Joe was really mad," Ralph kept repeating.

"I know, Ralph. I know."

The morning was turning warm, and Steve turned the air conditioner on. His cell phone buzzed, signifying that he had a message. He pulled it out of his pocket and checked it. It was Alec. "Just checking in. Let me know when Nori is settled into Flower Cottage."

That was all. He'd call Alec later. He had a few more messages, he noticed. Four of them, to be exact. All of them were hang-ups. The caller ID identified them as coming from Marlene's Café. When he got her on the phone, Marlene said, "Sorry, Steve, I wasn't trying to phone you. I'll ask Roy when he comes in, but I don't think so."

A silver fox darted out onto the road in front of them and disappeared into the woods.

In no time they were pulling into the driveway that led down to Flower Cottage. When they got there, Bette came out and gave Nori a hug. A soft breeze was blowing over the garden. This would be a good place for Nori. Already he could see her physically relax. She seemed so thin to him. He remembered that she had barely eaten the chicken pie last night.

At Flower Cottage, Ralph carefully removed his

shoes and placed them side by side on the porch. "Gotta weed the garden," he said. "Gotta get ready to weed the garden."

Before he left Nori, Steve pulled a package of red licorice out of his pocket and handed it to her. She grinned and took it.

"Licorice," she said. "You think it cures everything, don't you?"

"Sometimes it does," he said.

He fought the overwhelming urge to take her in his arms and kiss her right there. But Bette's arm was still around Nori. He wasn't sure a group hug was what he had in mind for right then.

"Thanks." Nori smiled at him. "I'll be fine here, Steve. Thanks . . . for everything. For believing in me. For not thinking I'm crazy." She reached out and touched his bare arm, and it was like an electric jolt. This was the first time she'd done something so tender.

Bette seemed to take the cue and let go of Nori. "Well," she said. "I'll head inside. Do you like chicken soup? I'm making some homemade soup for lunch and you look like you need some nourishment on a day like today."

"That would be nice," Nori said quietly. She clutched her nylon jacket around her, and Steve wondered how she could be cold on such a warm day. This was the same jacket she'd worn when he'd rescued her, a pale blue zip-up jacket made of ripstop nylon, with darker blue piping around the collar. She wore no makeup, and, without it, she looked pale but not unlovely.

"I'll be back soon. I have to go back to Trail's End to meet Alec," he said.

"I would like to go back to Trail's End tomorrow morning. I know you're not the police so maybe you don't know these things, but do you know if that would be all right? I have someone coming out to change the locks," Nori said.

"Tomorrow's Sunday."

"I said it was an emergency."

"I was going to ask you to come to church with me."

"Well." Nori opened her mouth and closed it. "I haven't been to church in such a long time, maybe I should go. My girls go all the time. They seem to like it. Hmm. Maybe I could call the locksmith and see if he could come out in the afternoon."

He smiled, thinking of sitting with her in church tomorrow. Maybe that's what they both needed, to bask in the worship of God. Him, because he needed to trust again, needed to be honest about his past, her because she was dealing with so much confusion and pain.

"But!" She put her hand up.

"What?"

"I have nothing to wear. I just . . ." She looked down at her backpack. "I would have to go back to Trail's End and get some clothes. I only have jeans and shorts and tees."

He grinned. "Then you don't know Maine very well." He opened his arms wide. "You see this? T-shirt? Shorts? Sandals? This is what I wear to church."

"Okay then. You've convinced me. I'll come. But just be warned. If I flee halfway through, just let me, okay?"

"Deal."

When they parted, she couldn't believe that she had agreed to do the one thing she had said she would never do again after Marty died—and that was go to church.

FOURTEEN

Bette took Nori upstairs to her room, which turned out to be a sunny, many-windowed space that overlooked the lake and grounds. Below her there looked to be tangled masses of wildflowers, but a closer examination revealed them to be well-tended flower beds. Nori felt safer already. As she looked out of her window she realized that this was exactly the kind of space she wanted to create out at Trail's End—peaceful, safe, full of flowers.

Down in front was the lake. She looked, but she couldn't see Trail's End from this end of the lake. Twin Peaks Island was right in the way.

Nori put her backpack on a chair, noting the four-poster bed, the floral spread, the chintz curtains, the chairs covered in fabric printed with tiny flowers. They reminded her of Molly Jones's miniatures. She also had her own private bathroom with a claw-foot tub, which was nice. The bathroom came with a basket of organic bath products. She was getting lots of ideas for Trail's End.

Down below, Ralph was already back outside in the sunshine. He wore big, white coveralls and was kneeling in the dirt and pulling up weeds.

Bette called from the bottom of the stairs in her lilting voice. "When you're settled in, come down and I'll give you a tour. I especially want to show you Ralph's flower beds. They are a treasure."

"It's very beautiful here," Nori told Bette as she made her way down the stairs. "This whole place is so lovely."

"And you're here on such a gorgeous day. The rain has really greened things up."

They walked down airy garden paths next to immaculate flower beds. Bette rented out several cottages and Nori found herself putting all the Trail's End ghosts behind her and talking about such things as advertising and keeping up a business like this. As they walked and talked Nori knew that Bette would be a potential mentor for her. In business and possibly in life, too.

If she even *had* a business after everything was over. She suddenly felt very sad and talked about this to Bette. She said, "How did it happen that out of all the places I could have bought, I end up in a house with an old ghost and a new crime?"

After a moment, Bette said, "I have to believe that God brought you here for a reason and a purpose. There are hundreds of other resorts you could have bought, but you picked this one. And Alec is a good man. He'll get to the bottom of this."

Nori remembered the way Alec had grilled her and wasn't so sure. She didn't say this, however. They were down along the beach in front of Flower Cottage. Nori loved what Bette and Ralph had done here. There were several well-kept wooden docks plus a quaint seating area built up with bricks and white rocks. Kayaks and canoes lined the shore. Bette also had two small day sailers, plus a few rowboats and a paddleboat.

"This is just what I want to do with my place," Nori said.

"Nothing big," Bette said. "No water-ski boats or anything like that. The people who come to my place seem to enjoy quiet pursuits. I have an extremely large guest library. I'll show you later. You may have noticed, I don't even have TVs in my guest rooms. It's not necessary, you know. But more and more people seem to like the Internet, so I do have that."

Nori nodded. She wished she had brought along a notebook to jot down all these ideas.

"I would say that you're welcome to take a boat out—it looks like it's going to be a beautiful day. You might even meet my neighbor Lark. I introduced you at the church social. She's a single gal, biologist. Comes here every summer to measure algae growth and some such. Fascinating person."

Nori nodded.

"And then on the other side of me are Greta and Irwin. They've been here longer than I have. Their grandchildren come every summer. Nice kids."

As they made their way back up the flagstone flower-lined path to the house, Nori felt the fatigue of the past few days settle in around her like a shroud. Suddenly the breezy, shady front porch with its cushioned white wicker furniture and hanging baskets of flowers looked so inviting. She would get her laptop, a glass of iced tea and take advantage of Bette's Wi-Fi. Bette said she was heading inside to get a bit of paperwork done before lunch.

She got out her laptop, but stopped before she e-mailed her daughters. What could she possibly tell them? All the bad news? She'd wait. Maybe when everything was figured out and settled—whenever that would be—she'd e-mail them.

Instead, she got out her cell phone and called Lisa. She leaned back in the wicker chair and they talked for an hour. Lisa insisted that Nori come and stay with her for a while. Nori said no, which got Lisa wondering aloud if this had more to do with the "wonderful Steve" than anything else. "I think you are quite smitten with that man," Lisa said.

"Maybe. I don't know. He's been so good to me through all of this."

"You *are* smitten. I want to know every detail of your dinner with him."

Nori promised, then added, "I'm sort of, I don't know . . ."

"Scared?"

"Scared to death," Nori admitted. "I'm going to church with him tomorrow."

"You're what?"

"Going to church."

"Church and dinner. This is serious."

They talked for fifteen more minutes. In the end Nori promised to call Lisa as soon as church was over and tell her all about it.

Nori hung up feeling hopeful. She thought about what Bette had said, that there was a purpose for her being here. Maybe, just maybe that purpose had to do with Steve.

It felt odd being in church after so long a time. Part of the reason Nori was afraid of going to church was that she was afraid it would be like Marty's funeral—somber, dark. Not that Marty's funeral had been somber and dark. She hadn't worn black, and some of his favorite praise music had been played and sung, but to her it was somber and dark.

When she had walked out of the church that day she knew it would be a long time before she'd be back. She had such a tenuous hold on God anyway. No matter what she did, she never felt she was good enough or did things right. Marty had been her strength. Marty had been her rock. And if God could take her husband like that, then God could not be trusted.

But this church service was not like the funeral. This church was upbeat and joyful, something that had been lacking in her life for so long.

And Steve was right. If she had worn a skirt she would have felt out of place. Her jeans were just fine.

The little white church was packed. Marlene and Roy were there, plus Bette and Ralph. A lot of the younger young people—the ones still in high school—were there. But the kids Selena's age were absent. Not Chase nor Joe nor Selena nor Blaine nor Meredith were there. Were they all mad at God about Heather's disappearance? If so, she knew how they felt.

Even though Steve said he went to church in shorts and tees, what he wore today was a nicely pressed golf shirt, clean khaki pants and sandals.

The music was new to her, but she had been out of it for almost two years, and things changed, new songs were written. Her eyes misted at the one familiar song she heard. The message was challenging. Steve took notes during the sermon. She found this endearing. For part of the sermon she watched him, this big man bent over his little notebook, intent on every word the pastor was saying.

The entire thing wasn't so bad. This is what she told Steve outside after church was over.

"See?" he said with that huge smile of his. "I told you it wouldn't be so bad."

They held hands as they walked to his truck. He drove her out to Flower Cottage, and she was a little surprised when he said goodbye so quickly. She'd half expected him to stay for lunch with her and Bette and Ralph.

He had to meet Alec in Shawnigan, he explained. She let go of his hand, disappointed.

"Tomorrow night," he said.

"Tomorrow night."

In the afternoon she met the locksmith out at Trail's End and watched while he put new expensive double dead bolt locks on her doors. This was something she should have done when she moved in.

No sooner had the locksmith left than Lisa showed up, driving her little compact car down her gravel driveway.

"Lisa!" Nori raced down from her porch in bare feet. "What are you doing here?" Nori hugged her friend. She had never been so happy to see Lisa in all her life.

"I've come for a little visit. You sounded rather drastic on the phone last night. I figured you needed a close-up friend, rather than a faraway friend. But I have to say I've been chasing all over Whisper Lake Crossing looking for you. I first went out to Flower Cottage and the woman there said you were here getting locks put in. Then I had to find someone to tell me how to get to Trail's End."

Nori grinned at her friend. Lisa was every bit the chic TV woman, from her perfectly coiffed highlighted hair to her dangling earrings and two-inch heels that she wore even now. She tromped up Nori's uneven wooden porch steps and continued, "I also brought something. A movie. It's in my bag. I figured we could use a chick flick popcorn night. Unless, of course, you're seeing Steve tonight? In which case I will wait up for you and listen to every juicy detail later."

"He hasn't called."

"Are you staying at that other place? The woman there, Bette, said you'd be back later."

"I'm actually thinking about staying here tonight. I've got new locks now. I'll be okay."

"Are you sure it's okay?"

"It's my house. Plus, I haven't seen any police here all afternoon, and there's no yellow tape. I think for the time being they're done with whatever they were doing. I'm sure they'll be back. They're going to do some kind of search out here. But I don't want to talk about that. What movie did you bring? I hope it's the new romantic comedy everyone's been talking about."

"*The Haunting of Trail's End.* I managed to find the VHS tape of that ghost documentary you asked about." She clunked her wheeled suitcase over the doorsill.

"Oh, wonderful," Nori said sarcastically. "Just what I need."

"It wouldn't be my favorite, either," Lisa said, delicately moving a wispy stray hair out of her eyes. "But it might give you a bit of knowledge about this place." Lisa stood in the huge living room and twirled around as she took in the high-ceilinged rock fireplace, the log walls, the hardwood floors. "I can see why you love it here.

Wow, Nori, wow! I agree. We have to stay here tonight."

"We shall. This *is* nice, isn't it?"

"So much potential."

"I'll call Bette. And maybe Steve. To find out if it's okay."

"If you're sure," Lisa said.

"I'm sure. I bought top-of-the-line locks."

When Nori called her, Bette said, "Are you sure? Lisa would be more than welcome at Flower Cottage. We've plenty of room, as you know."

"I know. And thank you so very much. You've been so kind. I left my backpack there with my toiletries. If I could come and get them tomorrow, that would be great. I've got another toothbrush here, so I don't need to drive in."

"Well, if you're sure, dear."

Her next call was to Steve. Oddly, he wasn't answering. She left a message.

"So," Lisa said. "I don't get to meet the famous Steve until tomorrow night."

"Maybe tomorrow morning. He could be out working here. But I never know from one day to the next what's happening. One day they're working, the next day this place is a crime scene."

She asked Lisa if she would mind sleeping on the foldout couch in the living room.

"Do I mind? This room is brilliant."

"Ignore the mess, though. I'm not totally

unpacked. If I'd known you were coming I'd have cleaned up a bit."

"It looks perfectly fine to me. More than perfectly fine. Now, can I have the grand tour?"

They talked while they walked. Nori showed Lisa her entire place—the kitchen, the huge living/dining area that she described as perfect for retreat guests. Lisa also admired Nori's master bedroom with the huge window facing the back, and the ensuite bathroom. When Nori opened the door to the massive room off the kitchen, Lisa said, "Wow, what was this room ever used for? You could have a church service in here."

The cabins were next and Lisa exclaimed over each cabin, pointing out its good features and its not so good ones.

The last place they went was upstairs to the loft. They were silent as they mounted the stairs. The desecrated picture of Marty was still there. Nori halfway expected that the police would've taken the picture with them, but it still sat on the easel. Fingerprinting powder was sprinkled all over the place.

"I don't want to stay up here," Nori said.

"Let's go down," Lisa said.

Nori pulled out some popcorn from the cupboard. Later, treats in hand, which also included a half package of red licorice, Nori turned on the movie.

The documentary began with an aerial view of

the Whisper Lake area. The announcer, whose deep voice seemed more suited to narrating horror movies than serious documentaries, began by saying that "Deep in the heart of a Maine forest nestled among ancient mountains lives a legend of a ghost that just won't die." He went on in that overly dramatic way and Nori understood why some—like Steve and Bette—said it was sensationalized.

The camera homed in on Trail's End. She saw the outside of her lodge and cabins and she wondered how the film crew had gotten permission from Earl to film this if he hadn't given permission for a police search.

The narrator said that this was what Trail's End looked like now. But it was not the same Trail's End as when Molly and James Jones had lived there. The camera shifted to an unrecognizable place and actors played the roles of Molly and James Jones.

Nori and Lisa ate popcorn and chattered as the story unfolded, which was good, because it lightened the mood. They watched the bear attack, saw Molly shooting the bear, which did not appear onscreen. Then the documentary cut to Molly sprawled on the body of her husband and wailing loudly, while the horror movie narrator went on. This part seemed overdone to Nori. It evoked no real emotion—not like reading the book.

Lisa was actually laughing out loud. "A bit over-the-top, wouldn't you say?"

In the next scene, Molly was seated at the kitchen table bent over tiny squares of paper while the reporter spoke about her "reclusiveness," and her "utter aloneness" after James's death. The documentary showed close-ups of her paintings, and Nori was struck again at the raw elemental beauty in them.

Finally, the documentary went predictably to the upside-down canoe, gently lapping against the rocks on the shores of Twin Peaks Island. "And her ghost, her unhappy presence, is said to roam Trail's End. Because of the untimely demise of her beloved husband, Molly Jones has laid a curse on the land, a curse that to this day has not been lifted."

There was nothing about bells, Nori noted.

Trail's End, according to the video, was abandoned for many years after that. Without care it quickly became run-down. In the 1960s a developer bought it and added the cabins and constructed the loft over the lodge. He rented it out for a number of seasons.

Even though it was somewhat remote, the narrator continued, it became a favorite vacation spot until the wife of the developer was killed in a "mysterious car accident."

"It wasn't a mystery," Lisa said, shaking her head. "I read a little about the history of the place.

The wife was an alcoholic and got in her car and drove it into a tree on the way out one night. No mystery there."

Nori pulled the throw blanket around her more securely.

After "this mysterious and unfortunate accident," it was bought by a family who had previously come for many years as renters.

The new owners added the dock and did further renovations. It was finally sold to Earl Bannister. The narrator made much of the fact that shortly after he bought the place, Bannister fell, badly injuring his back, and experienced ongoing back problems. "Did the unhappy ghost of Molly Jones have something to do with that?" the narrator asked.

"What a bunch of baloney," Lisa scoffed. "All of this is just coincidence. I mean, look at the number of times you fall around your house in the course of a couple of years. Do you call it being cursed?"

Nori shrugged. "But you have to admit," she said, "the movie may be weird, but he makes a good case for ghosts, and in particular my ghost."

Lisa leaned her elbows on her knees, looked thoughtfully at Nori for a moment.

"I don't know much about ghosts, Nori. I admit that. But I remember when I was a kid. I remember we were always told how dangerous it was to play with stuff like Ouija boards. But really, in your case I think the whole thing is pretty much hogwash. Didn't it strike you as such?"

"But what if it's real?"

"What if it's not? Why not go with that hypothesis for a while? What if it's not?"

Nori looked away from her friend. Because if it wasn't a ghost, then it was something way more sinister.

FIFTEEN

The following evening at six, Steve came to Trail's End to pick Nori up. Gone were the rumpled work jeans, the T-shirts, the flannel shirts. Gone were even the golf shirt and khakis that he wore to church. Tonight he had on a blue pin-striped button-up shirt and pressed pants. Nori had spent the afternoon like a schoolgirl getting ready for her first date, and trying not to make too big a deal of it. "It's just dinner," she kept saying to Lisa.

"Just a dinner? I don't think so. I hear the way you talk about him. I'm so pleased for you. I can't wait to meet him."

"Will you find enough to keep yourself busy alone here?"

"Of course," Lisa had said. "I've got a good book to read, plus you've got a pile of movies, some of them dreadfully romantic. I'll find enough and I'll be thinking of you and rooting for you."

"Keep the doors locked," Nori told her.

When Nori introduced Lisa and Steve and watched them shake hands, it struck her as strange. Lisa and her husband, Thomas, plus Nori and Marty often visited together and even took trips together. Marty and Thomas had been close friends. It wasn't until after Marty died that Lisa and Nori became close friends on their own.

After the funeral, Lisa told her, "I am not going to lose you as a friend. I'm going to do what it takes. It means we'll have to work at it, but I'm determined."

She had kept her word. Nori didn't know how she would have gotten through those early months without Lisa and Thomas.

At the door tonight, Lisa had given her friend a hug and whispered, "Not that you need my approval, but I approve."

Outside, Steve held the car door for her. "This is a beautiful car," she said, when he was seated behind the wheel. She took in the plush leather of the seats in the Volvo.

"It's not mine," he said, turning in her driveway and heading out. "It belongs to Bette. I figured this would be a bit nicer than my old pickup," he added.

"Your old pickup is fine, though. It's sort of like mine."

"A good vehicle for the Maine woods."

"Unlike this one," she said, as the car lurched and bumped over a prominent tree root. Steve drove it slowly, carefully.

"I'm still not totally sure you and your friend should have stayed at Trail's End last night. If I had been here, I would've made sure you stayed at Flower Cottage."

She put her hand on his arm. "It was fine. Nothing happened."

He frowned slightly. "I'm just not sure . . ."

"And I got new locks on the whole place. Really good ones."

"Excellent."

"So what did you do all day? I wasn't sure whether you'd be working here or not."

His face darkened for an instant. "I spent the day with Alec."

She turned to him. "The whole day?"

He nodded and the set of his mouth was grim.

"Anything new?" she ventured.

"Not sure."

"Do they know what happened to my painting?"

He shrugged. "No one knows anything. It's all speculation at this point." He hesitated. "And Alec isn't telling me everything he's thinking."

She nodded. She knew that Alec and Steve were friends. But she also knew the police didn't share their information with civilians, even if the civilians were close friends.

From the way he wasn't looking at her when he talked, she got the idea that Steve didn't want to talk about this. And maybe she agreed. He stared at the road ahead and cranked up the air conditioner a notch. He seemed nervous and she wondered why.

"You're not too cold, are you?" he asked.

"Not me. I can't believe the difference in the temperature once you get away from the lake."

"Did you have a nice time with Bette and Ralph?"

"Yes. It was a wonderful place. So beautiful."

"She's special."

After a while he said, "I wish you would have stayed there."

Did that account for this sudden dark mood? "I was fine, Steve, really."

"I admire your spunk," he said.

"You do?"

He nodded.

He pointed out various landmarks after that. She found him easy to talk to tonight. There weren't as many quiet spaces in their conversation. And those that were began to feel more comfortable. He was just concerned about her. They were clearly becoming more confident around each other. She liked that.

They had finally reached their destination. A sign out front read The Log Cabin. It was on the other side of Whisper Lake from Trail's End and overlooked the lake's western shores. It came recommended by Alec, Steve told her.

"Is Alec married?" she wondered aloud.

"No."

"I wonder why not."

"Guy just can't seem to settle down."

"Too bad."

"I think there was some great love in his life a long time ago. He doesn't talk about it."

"Sad." Maybe that accounted for his wariness around her.

"He doesn't believe me." She said it rather quietly. "About the ring, I mean. Does he think I'm crazy?"

"No one thinks you're crazy."

Steve took her hand as they walked up the flagstone path to the restaurant. She liked the way her hand felt in his. Steve told the waitress he wanted someplace private and they ended up being the only ones out on the deck.

"There are beavers and moose down there," the waitress told them. "You might be able to see a moose if you're lucky."

Over appetizers of battered shrimp, he said, "One of the reasons I wanted to be out on the deck was because I think it's time I told you about myself."

She dipped a shrimp into sauce and looked across at him and waited. He seemed to take a long time to begin, which gave her time to really look at him. He had an even-featured, pleasant face. His blue eyes sparkled. His light hair was shorter, she noticed, and she wondered if he'd gotten a haircut for this occasion.

Finally he said, "I used to be a sort of cop."

"Okay." She cocked her head to the side.

He was silent.

She waited.

He went on. "I wasn't an ordinary cop. I was in the military on a special task force to bring down terrorists. I've been lots of places . . . seen a lot of things, done a lot of things."

She put down her shrimp. "You mean," she said, "you were a spy or something?"

He nodded and her eyes went wide. He said, "Sort of. I would be away for long periods of time. My wife couldn't know where I was. That was part of it. She couldn't handle that. She couldn't handle the not knowing. It wasn't fair to her or to my son, especially my son. I ended up shutting them out."

She watched him without saying anything. She got the idea that this was difficult for him to talk about. They stopped talking while their appetizers were cleared away and neither spoke until their main courses were set down in front of them. When the waitress was well away, Nori looked at her lobster-stuffed chicken, then back at Steve.

He shifted in his chair. "When my wife left, I fell apart. I'd had more than my share of years in the military so I quit and came here. I lived in a cottage on Bette and Ralph's property for a while. Bette has been like a mother to me. She brought me back to myself and to faith in God. My friend Alec was also there for me. Between the two of them I survived." He had not picked up his fork to eat. Neither had she.

Nori moved her head from side to side. "I'm so sorry. How did you get to be such good friends with Alec?"

"My former unit commander wanted to talk with me about something. He didn't have my number, and I guess he thought the quickest way to get a hold of me would be through the sheriff's office. We've been friends ever since. I do some ad hoc work for him from time to time."

She carefully cut a piece of chicken with her fork. "That's why you're so interested in Trail's End. You worked with Alec about those kids who went missing."

He nodded slowly. "My former employment is not something I talk a lot about. I just thought you needed to know. Only a few special people know that I was in the military."

"So, I'm special?"

"Yes," he said, pausing. "You're very special."

Steve looked out on the lake and for a moment he seemed to emotionally move away from her. Obviously, it took a lot for him to tell her things. Maybe there would be a time when he could tell her more. She would wait for him.

A moment later he seemed to be back with her and smiling. It was the sort of moment where she expected him to pull out licorice.

They ate while the sun set behind them and cast red slivers onto the lake. He said, "What about you, Nori Edwards?"

"What about me?"

"I don't know a lot about you."

"Yes, you do," she countered. "You were standing right there when Alec asked me every question in the book about me and my daughters and Marty. You know everything."

"I know the facts. I don't know you."

She found herself drawn into his smile. "My life is pretty boring. Raised by a normal Christian family. Married young, childhood sweetheart. He was an artist, actually, on his way to great fame and fortune when he died. Two kids, twins, great girls. I've basically been a stay-at-home mom all these years while dabbling in painting." She looked up into his gentle face and wondered if his nose had been broken in military police work.

"You do more than dabble," he said. "You're very good. You said you paint murals? You mean those big pictures on the sides of buildings? Tell me about that."

Now that the conversation had shifted to her, he was eating his meal.

She said, "I've had some fun projects. It's not all outside work. Once I was hired to paint a blue whale on the upstairs bedroom of a fifteen-year-old girl. Another time I had to paint the New York skyline at night in a huge, luxurious bathroom in a house in the country. Seems the wife used to live in Manhattan and missed it. But—" she looked down into her chicken "—I haven't done a mural in a long time. Not since Marty died. That was an awfully hard time for me. I thought I was going to break, that I was going to shatter into a million pieces. So I gave up painting."

His smile was sad and soft. "Did you see a counselor or anything?"

She shook her head. "You have to understand, I was so mad at God. I shook off anybody's attempts to help me. After Marty died, I sat in a chair for three days." She looked up and into his blue eyes. "I'm going on and on. You have obviously had it worse, and I'm going on and on."

He touched her hand. "It's not a contest, Nori."

After dinner they held hands and walked in easy camaraderie along the lakefront. Their conversation moved from the hard places to favorite books and movies. It turned out they had similar likes in some things. But while they chatted, she wondered what had happened in the military to cause such sadness on his face. What had happened to him? She wondered if he would ever tell her. By the time they were on their way home they were talking about God.

Just before they hit the gravel road to Trail's End, they passed a car going the other way quite fast, too fast, for the narrow roads. Steve swerved to avoid it.

"Crazy drivers," he muttered.

Halfway down the stretch that led to Trail's End, they were making plans for their next time together. "One thing," he said, looking over at her. "I'd appreciate it if you kept the military thing quiet."

She studied him. "Okay."

"Even with your friend Lisa."

"I understand."

When they got to her lodge, she was pleased to see lights on all over. Around the sides of the closed blinds was the blue flicker of the TV screen. Good. Lisa was in there watching a movie.

He came around and opened her car door for her. When she rose to get out, he placed his hands on her shoulders and drew her to him.

"My best friend's right inside," Nori said into his ear. "She'll be coming to the window right now. She would've heard us drive in."

But his hands were on either side of her face.

"Then let's give her something to talk about, okay?" And he leaned down and gently held her and kissed her.

They walked arm in arm to her door, the fireflies consorting about them like a rainbow of diamonds just for them. At the door, he pulled her even closer and kissed her again.

"You are extremely special, Nori Edwards."

"And you, too. Oh, wait . . . ." She backed away.

"Wait, what?"

"I left my shoulder bag in your car. My bag from Flower Cottage is still in your car. Thanks for picking it up for me by the way."

"I'll get it for you. Just wait."

She leaned against the door of her house, hugged her arms and wished this night could go on forever.

It was taking him an awfully long time to fetch her bag, and when he finally carried it up to her with both hands he was not smiling. In fact, he looked downright angry. "Steve?" she said, moving forward, hoping he would kiss her again. Instead, he thrust the bag into her waiting hands and turned away from her, and she watched him walk stiff-legged to the car.

What was wrong? She put a hand to her lips where he had just kissed her.

"Steve?" she called again, but he was already driving away.

"So?" Lisa said, from her nest of blankets on the couch. "How was Mr. Wonderful?"

"Wonderful." Nori sat down on the couch next to her friend. Lisa grabbed the remote, paused the DVD and turned off the television. Nori went on. "We had a wonderful meal. We talked and talked. He even kissed me. We seem to have this neat sort of communication. It's like we really connect."

"Then why don't you look happier?"

Nori reached for a handful of popcorn that she really didn't want from a bowl on the coffee table. "It was just the last five minutes. He went back to get my backpack—" she hefted it onto her lap "—and he took a really long time. Then when he brought it up to me on the porch, he had changed entirely. He's such a strange man. . . ." She thought about his time in the military. Maybe that accounted for this.

"Maybe he just got a bad phone call."

Nori nodded and ate her popcorn. "That had to have been it. It was like I was being shut out. But . . ." She rose. "I won't obsess. It was nothing that had anything to do with me. He'll call me tomorrow and everything will be okay. Let me get my pj's on and I'll join you. What were you watching?"

"You've Got Mail."

"Oh, I love that one. I'll be right back."

As Nori was making her way to the kitchen, Lisa called out, "I forgot to tell you. Some girl named Selena was just here."

Nori turned. "Selena? She came here?" She thought about the car they had passed on the way in. "What did she want?"

"She wanted to see you. She seemed very upset that you weren't in."

Nori came back into the living room. "I can't believe she drove out here. That girl barely talks to me. She's a waitress at the café. What did she want?"

Lisa pulled the knit throw over her shoulders. "She kept asking if you were okay. She kept asking that over and over. 'Is she okay? Is she okay?'"

Nori puzzled. "Am I okay? That's weird."

"I told her I would pass on the message."

Nori looked at the clock over the mantel. "Does she want me to call her?"

"She didn't say that."

"Well, I can't call Marlene and Roy's at this hour. Did she give you a cell phone number?"

Lisa shook her head.

Nori paced a bit, feeling restless. Selena wanted to know if she was okay? What was that about?

SIXTEEN

One of the first things Lisa said to Nori the following morning was, "Have you looked him up online?"

Nori was barely dressed, hair tousled, and Lisa, already showered, had on a pair of capris and a jaunty sweater. She looked marvelous first thing in the morning and Nori told her so. The truth was, despite herself, Nori hadn't really slept well. She kept going over her time with Steve, that kiss, and then the sudden shift in his demeanor. She kept telling herself it was nothing. He would call her this morning and all would be well. Yet, she couldn't shake the fact that something was really wrong. Maybe he'd gotten a cell phone call. Maybe they'd found something about Heather and Scott. But Steve would have told her that. Maybe it had something to do with his ex-wife. Maybe during that time in the car, he'd gotten a phone call from her, or about her. Maybe he would tell her about it today. He'd come over, apologize for running off like that, and then tell her all about it.

There, she was obsessing again. She finally managed to ask, "Looked up who?"

"You're kidding me, right? You have a wonderful date with a wonderful guy and you haven't even checked him out on the Internet?"

"I don't have Internet here."

"Well, duh, my friend. You have somehow managed to e-mail me and your daughters. Come on. Get dressed. Let's go into town. I have to get back home by this afternoon. Let's find some free Wi-Fi and look him up."

"Marlene's Café."

"Great. I'll get to meet the famous Marlene."

"And if Selena is there, I'll ask her what she wanted."

Nori showered, dried her hair and pulled on ankle-length cotton pants and a knit shirt, and Lisa followed her in her own car so she could head for home after breakfast.

When they got to Marlene's Café, the closed sign was firmly in place on the front door. Nori parked in front and went up to the café windows and peered inside. All was dark. She went back to Lisa's car. "I have no idea why it's closed. She's always open by now. This is weird."

Lisa leaned out of her car window, her arm on the steering wheel. "I'm so disappointed. I wanted to meet your friend."

Nori looked up and down the street, feeling a vague unease that she couldn't measure and couldn't identify. "There's always next time, I suppose. There are some good places we could go to in Shawnigan."

"Lead on."

They chose a café on the main street in Shawnigan and Nori kept comparing the runny eggs and dry toast to Marlene's muffins. They didn't measure up. But at least the place had Wi-Fi. Nori put Steve Baylor's name into a search engine and came up empty.

Lisa expressed surprise. "Are you sure you have his name right? Everyone's on the Internet. There's always some little tidbit of information about everyone."

"Not unless Steve Baylor is an eighteen-year-old Australian surfing champion."

Nori wasn't surprised at all. Because of his former job, a fact she couldn't share even with her best friend, Steve had successfully kept himself under the Internet radar. She wondered idly whether Steve Baylor was his real name. Oh, why was she having all these doubts when he had kissed her the way he had?

They talked more. Lisa promised to come back with Thomas next time. "We'll stay in one of the cute little cabins."

"Nonsense. You'll stay with me in the lodge. Just wait until you see how I get it fixed up."

Before she left, Lisa hugged her and said, "Despite all the bad things, Nori, maybe coming out here has been good for you."

On the way back to town, Nori's cell phone rang. She smiled down at the caller ID before she picked it up. "Hey, Steve," she said before he could get a word in. She needed to talk this way. She needed to pretend that everything was completely okay. "I was going to call you. Lisa just left. We had a great time. And I had a nice time last night . . . Steve?"

"Where are you?" His voice was a growl.

"On East Bay Road. Lisa and I had breakfast in Shawnigan. We went to Marlene's and it seemed to be closed. I've never seen it closed, so we decided to drive to Shawnigan. It's on Lisa's way home anyway."

"There's a good reason for Marlene's being closed."

Nori was taken aback. "What?"

"Selena is missing."

"What?"

"Marlene checked Selena's bed this morning and it hadn't been slept in. She's called all of Selena's friends and no one knows where she is."

"What happened?"

"Don't play games with me, Nori. I've had it with games." Nori's intake breath was sharp. She didn't know what to say.

"Selena came out to Trail's End last night. In fact, I think hers was the car we passed," Nori said. "Lisa said she came to the door and asked for me. When Lisa told her I was out, she left."

Up ahead was a viewpoint turnoff and Nori pulled into it to continue her conversation. Her head was beginning to hurt. She wasn't understanding this.

"Selena asked Lisa if I was okay. I can't figure

it out . . ." But her words died on her tongue when she remembered. She said, "Steve, I was really sick the night after we ate the potpies. Could there have been something wrong with the meat? Maybe Selena knew something and was trying to tell me? Maybe there was something about the chicken. Were you sick that night?"

"Oh, that's convenient."

"Steve, you are totally confusing me. What's going on?"

"I don't know, Nori. You tell me. You tell me."

"Steve?"

"Where are you, Nori?"

She told him.

"Will you stay there? I need to talk to you. Will you not run off this time or make up a hundred different stories?"

"I'll stay here, and I won't make up a hundred stories because I never made up any to begin with. And I don't know what you're talking about. You're scaring me," she said, but he had already hung up.

She got out of her truck and leaned against it, her arms wrapped around herself. Down below, the vast blue of Whisper Lake was spread out in front of her. She felt cold all over. Selena was missing. Steve was angry. And she understood none of it.

A million things rushed through Steve's mind as he drove his truck to the lookout point. He had let himself trust and he had been betrayed. Again. You'd think he'd learn.

It started with that Sunday afternoon telephone call from Alec. His friend had told him that a cursory examination of the bells revealed that they were new bells and had been recently painted. Nori painted. "You figure it out," Alec had said.

"It couldn't be her," Steve had said.

But that wasn't all. Alec told Steve that a gift-shop proprietor reported selling five little white plain bells, plus one larger brass bell, to a woman fitting Nori's description.

"That wasn't Nori," Steve had said on the phone. He still refused to believe that.

"Why are you so sure of this?" Alec challenged.

"Because I know Nori, that's why."

"You *think* you know Nori. How long have you actually known her? A week?"

"You said it yourself, her police check came up clean."

"And you know how reliable that can be."

"I'm coming into Shawnigan. I want to talk to the eyewitness," Steve replied.

That afternoon Steve and Alec met the woman who ran Lakeside Scrapbooking and Gifts. Nori was described right down to the nervous way she had of taking big chunks of her hair and holding them out for a second before shoving them behind her ears.

"Height?" Steve had snapped.

The proprietor, a matronly, nervous woman who wore her jeweled glasses on a chain around her neck, indicated by a sweep of her hand.

"Wrong," Steve had growled to Alec. "Too short. That wasn't Nori."

Alec had taken him by the arm and led him out and away from the gift store. "Get a grip, buddy."

After that he had spent the rest of the day in his workshop working on the chair, certain that Alec was wrong. For whatever reason, Alec had it in for Nori, and Steve didn't know why.

Of course the woman who wasn't Nori had paid by cash. They were not so lucky as to have a credit card receipt that could be traced.

Other things tumbled through his mind as he drove out toward the lookout now. Bette had called her "emotionally fragile." He, himself, had seen her unsteady on her feet. By her own admission she had taken sleeping pills. What if it wasn't just sleeping pills? What if she was some sort of an addict? Could it be that there was no one out there trying to frighten her? Could it be that this was something Nori was doing to herself? But why?

Stop it, Steve, he told himself as his truck hit a pothole. *And slow down. You're driving too fast.*

He was used to people lying to him in the military. He could usually tell when somebody was telling the truth and when somebody was lying. It was one of the things he was good at. And he had to admit he hadn't seen it coming with Nori. If she was lying, then she was good. She was really good.

He was falling for her and it was funny what the mind did. But last night he knew for sure.

Throughout the evening he had meant to ask Nori about the bells. But the stars, the sunset on the lake, the dinner, the kiss—yes, the kiss—had put all of these questions and concerns to the very back of his mind.

Alec was wrong. Someone had bought bells, that much was obvious. Someone who knew the story of bells. But not Nori. She was an innocent. She was not a stalker. Someone was stalking *her.*

But last night, after he had gone back to his car to get her bag, he had seen the proof. There was a side pocket on Nori's bag, and as he grabbed it from the floor the clasp had came undone. Two things had fallen out—a permanent black marking pen and a receipt. In the overhead dome light he could see that the receipt was from Lakeside Scrapbooking and Gifts for six bells. The receipt indicated that it had been a phone order and the bells would be picked up by Scott Gramble. Why he didn't confront her right there and then he didn't know. He had put the receipt in his pocket, and hadn't even called Alec.

Instead, he went to bed and didn't sleep. All night long he was trying to come up with scenarios. How was she connected to Scott? Were they related? That was certainly possible. Could she be his big sister? Could she be his mother? Maybe he was her much younger lover? He thought about Julie and her ten-years-junior husband. The thought disgusted him.

Nori was not here for her daughters. She was here for Scott.

The lookout was just up ahead. Nori was leaning against the cab of her truck, hugging herself. His heart jolted and he took in a long breath.

He had told her so much about himself. Things he'd never even told Alec or Bette.

Was she trying by her wiles to uncover secrets? Could this possibly have to do with his military service? Was Scott Gramble after secrets? Maybe this situation had a wider scope than he thought.

She straightened when he drove into the viewpoint. There was confusion on her face and it looked as if she'd been crying.

He parked his truck and got out. There was a stiff breeze blowing now and, way below, Whisper Lake was dotted with whitecaps. Her movements toward him were slow and tentative.

She looked so beautiful to him he wanted to forget everything he knew about her, everything that Alec had speculated, and just gather her into his arms and take her away to some desert island where they could be happy and live together forever. The sun shone down on the freckles on her nose as she approached him, eyes red.

"Steve?" She swallowed, took a chunk of hair in

her hands to keep it from blowing in her face. "I'm worried about Selena."

"You should be." He spit out the words like venom. What made him so harsh? So hard?

She backed away, let her hair go to blow in front of her face. A cloud moved in front of the sun and it was suddenly colder. She kept hugging herself. They were the only ones at the lookout.

He reached into his pocket and, before he was able to remove the plastic evidence bag containing the receipt and the black marking pen, she tried a tentative smile. "Red licorice?" she asked. "Didn't you say that made everything better?"

He glared at her. "Don't make fun of me, Nori."

"I'm not. I'm . . ." She bit her lower lip. Her eyes swam with tears. "Steve, I thought we had a good time last night. I . . ."

"I thought so, too. I thought so, too."

"Then what's wrong?"

"It's this . . ." He showed her the bag. She stared at the receipt with Scott Gramble's name, and at the black marking pen. "What is this?" she asked.

"This fell out of your backpack last night when I went to get it for you."

She looked at it and up at him. "What? I have no idea what this piece of paper is for and why they were in my backpack."

But Steve wasn't finished. "A woman with your description was seen picking up these items from a gift store in Shawnigan."

"Scott Gramble—isn't that the boy who disappeared?"

"Nori, who is Scott Gramble to you? Why are you protecting him? Is he your brother? Your son?"

She stared at him. She opened her mouth to say something then clamped it shut. "I have absolutely no idea what you're talking about, Steve. I don't even know who Scott Gramble is!" She took a chunk of her hair and held it off her face. "Does this have something to do with Selena?"

"We don't know."

She was backing toward her truck. "I don't see how you can think this has anything to do with me. I thought you knew me." The tears were clearly flowing now.

She opened the truck door. "First of all, I can't believe you would look in my backpack, and second of all, I can't believe you would think I had anything to do with this. I don't know what's going on."

"Nori, where are you going?"

"I don't know. Back home. Oh, wait, I don't have a home. Not in this town. Not where no one believes in me."

He watched her leave, vaguely wondering if he should pursue her. But now he needed to do what he should have done last night, and that was to take this receipt and pen to Alec.

SEVENTEEN

Nori had never felt so angry, so hurt. How could Steve act the way he did toward her? Did those kisses mean nothing to him? Did their close conversation mean nothing? Obviously it didn't. Was he even who he said he was?

There was only one thing left for her to do, and that was to leave. She had tried here, she really had. She was even going back to church and she was praying again. She could tell that God was beginning to take the hard places of her life and make them softer.

And now this.

How could Steve be thinking she had anything to do with Selena's disappearance? Why did he think she was related to this Scott person? She hadn't even known what had happened before she bought Trail's End. If she had, she wouldn't have bought the property.

She would go back to Trail's End, throw her things into a suitcase and drive to Lisa's. Lisa would take her in until she could get on her feet again. Later she would hire someone to pack up all her other stuff at Trail's End. Then she would put the place on the market.

As she made her way to Trail's End, her rage changed from open and fiery to a more manageable simmer. It was such a shame, such a loss. In the three weeks she had been here at Whisper Lake, the place had grown on her. When she thought about leaving Trail's End, she thought about how she would miss kayaking on the lake. She would miss sitting out on the porch with her morning coffee. She would miss the loft.

And she would miss Steve. Nori had really thought that this could work. Tears started again.

Halfway down her lane, she realized she had another choice. She could try to figure out what was going on.

But where to even start? She pieced together what she knew about Trail's End, Heather and Scott, plus all the things that had happened to her. It occurred to her, too, that better minds than hers had been pondering the missing kids for a while now and had come up empty.

But she had the trump card. She owned Trail's End. She could conduct her own "thorough search" on her own terms. She realized that she didn't know what she was looking for, but then, neither did the police. Instead of running, which would just prove her guilt, she would stay. She would prove herself innocent, and after that, and only after that, she would leave Whisper Lake forever. She would never have to deal with Steve again.

It's just not fair, God, she said, pounding the steering wheel as she drove.

But she had to stay rational. She couldn't cry. A

person, and not a ghost, had put those things into her backpack. Her backpack had been at Flower Cottage for two days. Anyone could have gotten in there and done that. She began making a mental list of suspects.

Trail's End was eerily quiet when Nori arrived. After Steve's recent accusatory remarks, she expected the place to be lit up with squad cars and police waiting for her.

She unlocked the heavy dead bolts with her key. All was quiet. She went up to the mantel over the fireplace and checked the box. Her ring was still there. She took it out and put it on. Then just as quickly she slipped it off. If she left it on she would be doing it for the wrong reason. She would be wearing it because Steve had hurt her and she wanted to get back at him. No. It was time she let go of Marty, even if there was no Steve in her future.

She sat down heavily on the couch and remembered that not so many days ago she and Steve had sat on this very couch, knees touching while they looked at photographs of his cupboards. She looked up and out the window and onto the wide wooden porch. That's where Steve had kissed her.

She wiped a lone tear away from her eye. Maybe a person is destined, she thought, getting up, for only one true love in their life. Maybe she had had her shot at happiness and Marty was it, and it was now over.

With a sigh she made her way into the kitchen. She had things to do. She couldn't dwell on sadness right now. From the corner of her kitchen table that served as her desk she grabbed a blank sheet of lined paper and a pen. At the top she wrote:

Things I know:
1. I own Trail's End.
2. There were parties at Trail's End.
3. Heather and Scott were last seen at a party at Trail's End.

Did she know the date of that party? No. Something so basic and she didn't know it. She couldn't look it up online. She wasn't getting satellite Wi-Fi for another couple of weeks. She stopped herself in her thoughts. Here she was still making plans for Trail's End. Didn't she know this part of her life was now over? She'd be gone long before any satellite guy could come out and hook it up.

She went back to her list. She tried to remember all of the times that windows had been left open and doors were unlocked. Nori had to admit that it went back to the first day she moved in. But when you're dealing with grief, anything out of the ordinary, you just chalk it up to stress, delayed grief, post-traumatic stress, whatever name you called it.

She made a detailed list then of every door or window that she could remember. It had been warm the day Steve had rescued her and she had left every window open. When they had gotten to the lodge in the rain, every window was closed. She wrote that down.

And then there were the bells—three of them now. New bells. New paint. This refuted the ghost theory if anything did. There was no ghost. She understood that now. Someone was pretending to be a ghost to frighten her.

She put her pen down. So far she had managed to fill three pages. She got up and walked to the window. A thought was coming to her, tenuous as fine thread. She needed to think. She was new here and not involved in the disappearance of the two kids, yet she was being drawn into it. "Why?" she said aloud. Who was trying to scare her away? Maybe whatever it was was here on the grounds of Trail's End.

Outside, dark clouds were gradually overtaking the sun and the lake looked like slate. The weather in northern Maine was fickle. The lake could be a torrent one minute then smooth as silk the next. That's where the ghost idea had most likely come from.

She thought about Selena, Blaine, Meredith, Chase, Joe and Connolly, and their strange reaction to her. It was almost as if they were frightened of *her.*

She wrote "chicken pies" on her list. Both times she had eaten Selena's pies she'd been sick. The first time it was almost like hallucinating. She remembered being up in her loft. It was as if sparkling paints and colors dripped off the tips of all five fingers.

The second time she had eaten part of a pie it was severe nausea. But that was the night she had seen the so-called ghost out on the lake. Was Selena trying to poison her? What would've happened if she had eaten the whole pie?

Nori put a big question mark on the paper. Then added another.

She got the rest of her uneaten potpie out of the fridge. She sniffed at it, afraid to bring it too close to her nose. Where does one take food items to get them tested for poisons? The police? But they didn't believe her. She left the container on the table.

Another thread was being pulled through the puzzling design of this mystery—the painting on the bells. She dimly remembered Marlene saying something about Chase painting pictures.

Could Chase have done this? Chase and Selena? Were those two trying to scare her away? She thought about Selena, almost gothlike, and the stoop-shouldered Chase. According to Marlene, Heather had been their friend. Maybe Heather and Scott had run off together and Chase and Selena knew where they were, and the clue to where they were was somewhere here at Trail's End. Maybe Selena and Chase were trying to protect their friends. She wrote that down and added a question mark.

It was time to go look for whatever it was.

She started with the huge barnlike room attached to the kitchen. This hall had only small windows near the ceiling. She had no idea who or why someone had built on a room of this size, but she had decided that someday it might serve as an art gallery.

She planned to remove the minuscule, grimy windows and put in large, airy ones. But for now, the place was filled with broken furniture, furniture pieces, boards, ladders, trunks, pieces of metal, insulation and cans of paint. So far she had gone through the stuff along the north wall and all she managed to come up with were about a dozen bags for the dump.

There was nothing like letters or diaries. What was she expecting? Clues handed to her on a silver platter? And speaking of silver platters, there was a terribly tarnished one on top of a pile of wooden trays. She took it down.

Nori rooted through more things. She decided that whatever it was she was looking for wasn't here.

The cabins were next. Steve had found the wallet in the first cabin so it was the first cabin she ventured into. Despite a couple of very short workdays, the cabin looked spiffy and clean and ready for a fresh coat of paint.

Again she chided herself for continuing to make plans about Trail's End when she knew she would be leaving. As soon as she could prove her innocence, she would be gone and the place would be put up for sale. The thought saddened her a little bit and she choked back a sob.

She examined each cabin, beginning with the outside structure, the foundation, and then ending up inside. She could find nothing.

Nori worked her way down the path. The first five cabins held nothing, at least nothing that she could immediately see.

In Cabin 6, on top of the small fireplace she found what looked like a diary. It was small, blue and held closed with three elastic bands. In the dim light from the dirty window, she looked through it. There were dates, words that had to be code words, colors and names. She flipped through, page after page, reading items like Royal Coach 523—16 IN, 2.2 pounds.

Did this have something to do with drugs? Is that what this was all about? The young people were using Trail's End as some sort of place where drugs were bought and sold?

She put the small book into her pants pocket and continued her search. Was this the evidence they didn't want her to find? There were no more books like that.

The only cabin that looked remotely different from the rest was Cabin 10, and that was another thing she was going to do. She would give all of the cabins real names.

Each cabin had a wooden porch, which ran the length of the cabin, attached to the front door. The porches weren't very big, but you could fit a couple of wooden chairs. Painted in primary colors, these would stand out.

The porch on Cabin 10 looked as if it had been removed from the cabin and then reattached. She could see where the paint had chipped.

She would add these findings to her notes. It was starting to sprinkle, so she made her way quickly to the lodge. Almost to the front porch of her lodge, she heard a truck coming down the lane. Was it Steve coming to arrest her for something? He used to be a cop, so maybe he could. Well, she would show him the drug book. She wondered that he had simply let her drive away from the roadside turnout. To her that proved the police didn't have enough to question her.

But it wasn't Steve's truck. She stood in the rain and waited. It was Joe's.

She didn't know Joe very well, perhaps had spoken to him only a handful of times.

He stopped and leaned out of his window. "Get in," he said.

"Joe," Nori said, approaching him.

"I said, get in."

"What for?" She looked at his thin, unsmiling face.

"Steve needs you."

She stood very still. Steve needed her and sent Joe?

She was getting a strange vibe from this whole exchange, and found herself unconsciously backing away from Joe's truck. "No," she said.

"Steve will die if you don't come." His voice was flat, lacking in emotion.

"What?"

"I said Steve will die if you don't come. Get in and I'll take you there." There was something about the way he was staring at her, unblinking. She had figured Chase and Selena were responsible for frightening her, but was it Joe? And why?

Joe opened his door. He was getting out of the truck. He was coming after her. She backed away quickly, so quickly that in her haste she caught her sandal on the edge of one of the uneven flagstones between the porch and the parking area.

She fell. Hard. She had fallen one way while her foot had landed the other way. The pain in her ankle shot all the way up her leg. She had cut her left knee on the rocks and it was bleeding.

"I'm hurt," she said, attempting to get up.

He offered his hand and she took it, though recoiling from his touch.

"I'll take you to the hospital after we see Steve. Get in the truck."

"No need," she said, wiping off her shorts. "I'll drive myself."

But he had grabbed her and was pulling her hands together behind her back. He pushed her roughly toward his truck. "I said get in."

"Okay, okay."

No matter how much she struggled, his grip on her became tighter. Her ankle hurt horribly, but there was nothing she could do except try to keep as much weight off it as possible. He had grabbed both wrists behind her and she realized with horror that he was binding them together with a plastic tie.

Despite his ranginess, he was incredibly strong. He shoved her into the passenger seat. She kicked him hard with her good foot.

He winced, but only slightly. "Don't do that. It'll just make it harder for you." His voice was monotone.

He pulled the seat belt across her. She could move her body a bit, but could not reach the door handle nor the seat belt release.

Nori struggled and screamed as loudly she could.

"No one will hear you out here," Joe said matter-of-factly.

He left her then and walked up the rocks to her porch. She watched as he dragged her kayak from under the porch. As soon as he got it out, he hefted it on his shoulder and came up around the other side of her dock. He put it into the back of his truck.

"What did you do that for?"

"Insurance." He got into the truck and started it. "So people will just think you're out in it."

"Where are we going?" she demanded. "People will see my kayak on the truck when we get to town. They'll wonder where I'm going."

"We're not going to town."

Instead of driving toward Whisper Lake Crossing, Joe turned and headed the opposite way. Nori had hiked this way, and she knew it was not a road for a truck. She said, "Are you in this with Chase and Selena? Huh? Tell me."

He didn't answer her.

It occurred to her that she wasn't dealing with someone who was entirely sane. She decided to tread carefully. He might tell her a lot if she worded her questions correctly. "What's going on? It's only fair that you tell me."

He did not speak.

The little notebook with all the notations was safe in her pants pocket. Her cell phone, however, was on her kitchen table along with the notes she had made.

A little farther on down the potholed road she tried again. "Tell me something, Joe. Did Selena put some sort of a hallucinogen into my chicken pie?"

He looked at her out of the corner of his eye.

"We didn't want to kill you, only to make you afraid so you would leave. We needed Trail's End for ourselves. It had to be ours. Ours," he emphasized.

"And Chase painted the bells, right?"

Joe said, "You're a smart lady. Too smart. That's why we have to get rid of you now. And Steve, too."

"This is about Heather and Scott, right?"

He turned to her viciously and said, "She betrayed me."

They hit a huge rut in the road and the truck went flying. Nori said, "You can't get much farther down this road than here."

But as soon as she had spoken, she saw a four-wheel quad parked in the center of the road.

"We'll go the rest of the way on that."

Nori saw this as a possible time to escape, but when Joe came around the truck, he held a pistol. She limped toward the quad as best she could, aware of his gun. He held her arms behind her and led her to the back of the quad. She complied. She looked longingly down the road they had come. She would have to think of some way to get out of here.

EIGHTEEN

Even though working with wood soothed him, Steve couldn't bring himself to go into his workshop. Nori's rocking chair was there, and sanding it and staining would make him think of her. Not that he wasn't thinking of her every minute anyway.

He and Chester were at the end of his dock in the spitting rain. He didn't care. Maybe the rain would wash away the mess he had made of everything. He had handled the whole thing with Nori very badly, very unprofessionally. He shouldn't have been the one to confront her about the receipt and the marking pen. He should have left that to Alec—which would have happened if he had given Alec the receipt last night. But Steve thought he could handle it.

Chester stood at his feet, gazing, it would seem, out at the water, too. His dog seemed to understand the gloom that his master found himself in.

During his previous night of no sleep, he had pretty much come to the conclusion that Scott had murdered Heather. Nori somehow knew Scott or maybe was related to him, and was now protecting him.

But questions remained. If Nori was protecting Scott or trying to cover up evidence at Trail's End, why would she go on and on about a ghost and bells and disappearing rings? To get the police off track? Wouldn't it be better if she just stayed quiet?

He had to admit his theory had a few holes.

And then there were his own feelings. He was in love. Obviously, that was clouding his judgment. If he was the commanding officer and someone under him pulled a stunt like Steve had by with-holding evidence, even under the pretense that he wanted to "scope out the suspect," the guy would be off the case so fast his head would spin. Steve had had no right to keep the evidence, much less run out to the viewpoint and confront Nori about it.

Rain splattered on the lake all around him. Alec had the receipt and the pen now, and they were part of the open investigation into the disappear-ances of Heather Malloy and Scott Gramble.

He didn't move, couldn't move. Way out across from the headland and past Twin Peaks Island was Trail's End. He stood where he was and tried to imagine what Nori would be doing now. And then stopped himself.

By sheer force of will he tried to eradicate all feeling from his mind, his heart and his body. He had done this before. This was how he kept con-trol—by not feeling.

He found himself praying then, making himself bow his head and give all of this to God. "I don't want to be like this," he prayed. "Even if it hurts, I need to be human. I can't go back to that place. . . ."

At his side, Chester whimpered. There was something he couldn't get his mind around, and that was Nori's reaction at the lookout point. He had been so upset with her—for lying to him—and upset with himself—for finally trusting, that he hadn't really noticed *her.*

There had been not a glimmer of recognition in her face. Her surprise, her confusion seemed absolutely genuine. Was that true? Maybe he needed to talk with her again, listen to her without jumping to conclusions.

"Chester, let's you and me try to figure this out, okay?"

Steve opened his truck door and Chester bounded in and sat waiting on the passenger seat, ears alert, tail wagging, awaiting adventure.

When Steve got to Trail's End, Nori's truck was there. That was a good sign. He would speak to her, and he would listen this time. Even if she knew Scott, he would give her a chance to explain herself to him.

He knocked on the door of the lodge. No answer. He went around to the kitchen door. Still no answer. He looked through the windows of the kitchen door. The kitchen was empty. There was a sheaf of paper on the table. But he couldn't see Nori.

He called Alec on his cell phone. Perhaps Alec had driven out here and Nori was, even now, answering questions at the sheriff's office.

"Is Nori with you?" Steve asked.

"Steve, I don't have enough on Nori to even question her."

"So she's not with you," Steve asked.

"Nope."

Steve went down the steps, and saw that Nori's kayak was gone. She had told him once the kayaking was a time when she got her thoughts together. There were fresh drag marks.

He went down to the lake and walked the length of her rickety dock, Chester scampering along beside him. He looked up and down the shoreline. He didn't see her, but that didn't necessarily mean anything. She could be paddling around Twin Peaks Island by now.

He headed back up to the lodge and tried her cell phone. He heard it ring from within her house. That was odd. Nori seldom went anywhere without it.

On impulse he tried her kitchen door. He was surprised to find that it was unlocked. Nori told him last night that she never went anywhere without taking her cell phone and securely locking her place up. "I don't even leave a window open, not a crack," she had said. "I don't care how hot it gets in the day."

He stepped hesitantly into her kitchen, Chester at his heels. He looked around. Nothing seemed amiss, but why had she left her door unlocked?

His attention was drawn to the sheaf of papers

on the table. Next to it was a pen. He picked up the papers and read the top handwritten sheet.

What I know.

These were lists and paragraphs in Nori's handwriting. As he sat down and read each line, it dawned on him how wrong he had been about her. How wrong they had all been. He read the last line, "Someone is stalking me and I don't know why."

He stood, holding the papers in his hand and looking out of the window. Was Nori in danger even now? Was she out on the lake in her kayak? He needed to find her.

Outside, Chester stopped and whimpered. He sat on the stone path in front of the steps and wouldn't move.

"What is it, boy?" Steve asked.

In front of Chester there were spatters of blood on the ground and fresh scuff marks leading down to the lake. He bent down and ran his forefinger over it.

"Chester," he said, rising. "Let's you and me go find Paul and his fastest boat on the lake."

Knowing Joe had a pistol in his belt, Nori was careful as she made her way from the four-wheeler down to the cabin. Her ankle was getting steadily worse, and each step hurt so much that it almost nauseated her. It had to be more than a sprain. It didn't look right.

When she stumbled, he said, "Move!"

"I can't go any faster." She was near tears from the pain.

The trail was filled with roots, rocks and debris, and the rain on her back was cold. She bent to scratch a bug bite and Joe ordered, "Walk straight. No funny business."

Nori recognized where they were, or thought she did. This was one of the many hunting cabins she had seen on her kayak trips. She knew this one because she had tried to get close to its shores and couldn't. The beachfront down below here was clogged with logs, water plants, mud and slippery rocks.

Even if she wanted to, she couldn't run away, not with her ankle the way it was. Behind her, Joe said in a clipped, even voice, "Up to the shack. Inside."

It was raining harder. Nori wished she could shove the wet hair from her eyes. "Why?" she asked. "Why do you want me here?"

Joe didn't answer.

She was in front of the cabin door and cast furious glances around her. She knew if she went inside, she would probably never come out. She tried to get her bearings. If her calculations were correct, this shack was about five miles from Trail's End. The trail was overgrown with trees and brush. No one would be able to come out here. The quad they were on had barely made it.

The walk would take hours with her ankle, even if she were able to escape.

"Open the door!" Joe said in a loud voice.

She looked over her shoulder, dumbfounded. How did he expect her to open the door when her hands were fastened behind her?

An instant later the door was opened from the inside by Chase.

"Chase!" she said.

He looked at her briefly, but his gaze quickly went down to the floor.

Joe shoved her forward and she fell onto a pot-bellied stove, which stood square in the center of the room. She groaned. The sky outside was black and inside the cabin was dim and chilly. She could barely make out the items in the room. A black chimney led up to the ceiling from the stove. There were some rickety chairs and a set of built-in cupboards along the right wall, with a grimy porcelain sink. A few canned goods were stacked on the shelves above the sink. There were two sets of bunk beds built into the other walls.

She heard whimpering behind her and turned.

"Selena!" Nori cried.

Huddled into the back corner of a bunk against the wall was Selena. Her hands and feet were bound and her mouth was covered with duct tape. She looked at Nori wide-eyed above her taped mouth. Strands of dark hair hung into her eyes.

Joe grabbed Nori and plunked her down on a

chair. He roughly cut off the plastic ties and then redid her hands in front of her. She gave a cry of protest when he bound her ankles together. She caught her breath again. When the pain momentarily lessened, she managed to breathe out, "What do you want with me? Why am I here?"

He said simply, "You were going to find the evidence."

They didn't know she had already found it. Nori thought about the small notebook tucked in the inside pocket of her pants—the notebook she was sure contained all the evidence the police would ever need.

If they found her dead at least they would find the notebook, put two and two together and arrest Joe and Chase.

It was drugs. She was sure of it now. Trail's End had been used as a place where drug business was conducted. Maybe it was even a meth lab, although she had seen no evidence of that. Somehow Heather and Scott were involved in the business.

"I know what's going on," Nori said. "I know all about the drugs. I know what Trail's End was used for. I knew it was you three who tried to get me to leave Trail's End."

Joe leaned against the far wall. He played with the revolver in his hand and Nori noticed that the fourth finger of his left hand turned in a bit. It was Joe's handprint she had seen on her loft window.

"You were in my loft," she said.

"Scoping it out," he said. "We had to."

"You destroyed my painting and took my ring."

"We gave it back."

"We, that's you and Chase?"

"And Selena." He indicated her with the movement of his head.

She asked, "Where are Heather and Scott?"

Selena was frantic and crying. Heavy tears made their way past her nose and down her cheeks and rolled over her duct-taped mouth. She made a sound like the mewling of a cat.

Joe came close to Nori then. His face was so near to hers that she could smell his cigarette breath. She turned away. "Dead," he said. "Like you will be."

He stood up. "I have to go move the kayak." He turned to Chase. "I'm putting you in charge. Don't blow it."

"Where are you going?" Chase asked. His voice was hoarse.

"Down to the lake where I'll let the kayak go. So when Nori turns up missing, people will think she died in the lake in this storm." He handed Chase a cast-iron frying pan. "If they give you any trouble, knock them out with this. Think you can handle it?"

"No gun?"

Joe laughed. "I'm not trusting you with a gun. I know you can be counted on. Because if you can't, you know what will happen." He made a motion like the cocking of a gun with his finger in Chase's direction. Then he left. They heard the quad start and the sound faded into the distance.

Nori thought about their situation. She looked at Chase, small and sad and skinny, holding a frying pan. She decided that if she tried to appeal to his reason, she might get somewhere.

"Chase?" she said quietly. "I know you're not a part of—"

"Shut up!" His voice was a cry. A cry for help?

Nori tried again. "Chase, I've seen the way you work. You guys did some amazing work out at my place. . . ."

"It's not your place."

"I'm afraid it is, Chase. But I know you're basically a good person. I can see it in your eyes. Why don't you at least take the duct tape off Selena's mouth. It makes it really uncomfortable and hard to breathe."

"I can't," he said. "She'll scream."

"No, she won't," Nori said, and on the bed Selena nodded rapidly.

"I'm not saying let us go, just let Selena breathe for a minute." She wanted to talk to Selena and get the girl's take on things.

He looked at Selena and a kind of softness came into his face. It was something Nori hadn't seen before. She saw him at that moment not as the skinny kid with a bad attitude, but as a boy who'd had a lot of hard life happen to him.

"It's okay," Nori said. "She won't scream."

He put the frying pan on the stove and went over and gently took the tape off her mouth. "But when we hear Joe, we have to put it back on," Chase said.

"She understands that," Nori said.

As soon as the tape was torn off, Selena looked up at Nori and her first words were, "I'm so sorry, Mrs. Edwards. I didn't want to poison you. I always put less morphine in the chicken pie than Joe told me to."

"Morphine?" Nori was taken aback. "Where did you get . . ." Then she remembered seeing Joe pick up the prescription for his father. "Joe took your father's prescription," she said, looking at Chase.

Chase nodded. "It was easy. Joe gave our dad plain aspirin, told him it was morphine."

Nori shook her head. "But why?"

Before Chase could answer, Selena said, "Chase, you have to let me go outside. I have to go to the bathroom."

He looked at her with new misery. "I can't. You heard what Joe said."

"Chase," Nori said. "That's inhuman."

He looked frantically from Nori to Selena then said, "Okay. But you have to promise—"

"I promise," she said.

He went and untied her bonds. After Selena left, he once again grabbed the frying pan and held it in his lap.

"You have to tell me what's going on," Nori said. "Does it have to do with drugs?"

"Drugs? No. What drugs?"

Nori thought about the notebook in her pocket.

"Joe has to kill you."

"Kill me, why?"

"For what you plan to do with Trail's End. Make it into a condo."

What was he talking about? Nori wondered.

"Joe said he heard you were going to dig up the place and put in a condo. Peach told us."

"Where did he ever get . . . ?" But she remembered that silly conversation with Peach. Peach had asked her if she planned to dig up the place and put in a condo, and she had come back with, "I wish."

She said, "What's down there? What don't you want me to find? Drugs?"

Chase shook his head. "Why do you keep saying drugs? It's not drugs. It's Heather and Scott."

"What!"

"Joe buried them. We don't know where. Somewhere at Trail's End. No one ever thought anyone would buy that place so the bodies would be safe and hidden there. We just wanted to scare you away. It was Selena who came up with the ghost idea. She knows about all these things."

Nori shook her head. "Chase, why did Joe kill Heather and Scott?"

"It wasn't just Joe." Selena was standing in the

doorway of the cabin. "It was all of us. All of us are equally to blame."

Nori stared at her dumbfounded.

Selena entered the cabin. "Joe tied me up and was going to kill me, too, because I was going to go to the police. I was sick of it all. You don't know how it is to have something like this hanging over your head for almost two years. I couldn't live with myself. Heather was my friend. After I put morphine in the second pie, I told Joe that I wasn't going to do it anymore. I was going to go to the police, no matter what. That's what I came out to see you about last night."

Nori stared at them. She seemed incapable of speech. What had happened?

Chase was talking now. "You don't understand." He held the frying pan and looked down at his running shoes. They were filthy and soaking. There were scratches on his face and dirt on his hands. He swallowed and his Adam's apple bopped. "Joe is my brother."

Nori said, "I'm guessing that Joe did this, not you. That's what I'm guessing. Am I right?"

Chase shook his head. "Not really."

"Why don't you tell me what really happened?" Nori was feeling chilled. Her ankle throbbed and she had to swallow to quell rising nausea, brought on by fear and pain.

Selena began. "We did a horrible thing." She was sitting on the couch hugging her knees.

"Especially because it was my friend. They both were."

Nori waited. The rain was coming down hard. She had no way of knowing how soon Joe would be back, but she figured that if she knew the whole story she might be able to help them get out of this.

Rain dripped onto the top of the stove from the place where the stovepipe went through the roof. Outside, lightning flashed and thunder shook the cabin. Everything felt damp.

Selena began. "Joe was mad that Heather broke up with him. Scott came from a bad family, but he was really a nice guy. He had this nice foster family and they showed him how to be a Christian."

Chase added, "He didn't even use his real name because he didn't want to be associated with his family."

"He made up a name," Selena said. "And when Heather met Scott, that was it. She was really ready to break up with Joe because she said that Joe was controlling and mean. He even hit her once."

"What happened at the party?" Nori asked quietly.

Chase said, "Joe didn't want to kill her. He only wanted to beat Scott up. Teach them a lesson."

"It was a crazy party and raining out. Just like now," Selena added.

Chase said, "Joe had his gun and he was aiming it at Scott, more like in fun."

Nori shook her head. How do you aim a gun at someone in fun?

Selena took it from there. "And then Heather started really freaking out and she came at Joe and by this time all of us were screaming and yelling. And I don't even know who came at Joe in the end, but the gun went off and . . ." Selena put her hands over her eyes. "It was so horrible. His face. It was all . . ." She sobbed for several seconds. "Scott fell into this clump on the ground in the mud, and Heather was really freaking out. It was so crazy and awful. All of us were there, Blaine and Meredith and Connolly, the whole bunch of us. And it was all crazy and everyone's screaming and yelling at Joe and telling him he had killed Scott, but he's saying no, that it wasn't his fault, it was Heather's because Heather was reaching for his hand. And so it was really Heather who killed Scott. And this makes Heather go even more nuts and she's clawing at Joe's face and he pushes her or someone pushes her really hard—I don't even know who. I think maybe it was someone just trying to push her away from Joe, I think. And she fell back really hard and hit her head. Heather didn't get up after that."

"It was an accident," Nori said finally. "It was a horrible, terrible thing that happened. But it was an accident. What happened then?"

Selena shook her head. "I can barely remember that part. I remember going back into one of the cabins. Scott had just gotten a stupid little plastic wallet for Heather, and I was holding it. I don't even know why. I end up putting it under the bottom leg of the bed. We were all in one of the cabins."

"I had to help my brother," Chase said. "We moved Heather and Scott out behind the cabin the farthest from the lodge."

"Cabin number ten," Nori said.

Selena added, "When Joe came back, he was like a different person. He told us we were all equally to blame. We had to make a pact. He told me to put up the Facebook message. And we had to act like nothing happened."

"Where are Heather and Scott now?" Nori asked.

Chase and Selena shook their heads. "We don't know. Joe went back and buried them, he said. They're somewhere there at Trail's End."

"We did all of the ghost things because Joe made us," Selena said. "Meredith went in and bought the bells because she looks the most like you, and even put Scott's name on the receipt and I put the receipt into your bag when you were at the café one day. That was just to scare you."

Nori thought about that. Meredith was about her height.

Chase said, "Joe made me paint flowers on the bells. You were supposed to think there was a ghost."

"So you would leave," Selena added.

Nori looked from one to the other. She thought about the kids, and the fact that a spurned and angry Joe had caused two deaths, and had somehow blackmailed or controlled all of the kids into believing that they were equally responsible.

"Untie my hands," Nori said. "I have something that might help."

Chase did so, and she took the little notebook out of her pocket. "What's this?" he asked.

"I found it in one of the cabins. I thought it had something to do with what happened. Joe didn't see it when he brought me here."

Chase picked it up and studied it. Then a slow smile spread across his face. Nori couldn't remember seeing him smile before. "This is nothing to do with anything," he said. "This is just some old guy's fishing diary."

"*Fishing* diary?"

"Yeah. My dad was a fisherman. That's why he wanted Trail's End. Because of fishing. You write what you caught and what kind of lure or fly you used to catch it. That's all this is."

Despite herself, Nori laughed out loud. Well, so much for her investigative skills. She sobered quickly. "You know what, guys? We don't have much time. We have to get out of here. Trust me. We can do this."

Her voice held more hope than she actually felt. In truth, she wondered if they really could make it to safety.

NINETEEN

Steve headed straight for the Whisper Lake Crossing Marina.

"Paul!" Steve yelled when he roared into where Paul was drinking coffee with a couple of his cohorts. "I need *Wild Lady*. Now!"

In a former life, Paul's cigarette boat had been used to run drugs off the Florida coast. Paul had bought the thing off the Internet, plugged up the bullet holes and repainted her. He sometimes joked that he'd redeemed *Wild Lady*, and turned her into a nice Christian lady. He often talked about changing her name.

"You need a wild lady?" Paul said, putting down his coffee. "I'm sure there would be plenty of females happy to oblige."

Steve was in no mood to joke. "Someone may be in danger out on the lake. She's in a kayak. I need your fast boat." *In danger?* How did he know that? He didn't. It was just a feeling. He'd read all that Nori had written. There was blood on the rocks in front of her lodge. Maybe someone had taken her at gunpoint and forced her into the kayak. Or maybe she'd seen a chance to escape and had gone by lake rather than by the road. It was more than a gut feeling; it was an ache in his gut that wouldn't go away.

"Be my guest, but I get to drive. No one drives *Wild Lady* but me."

"Let's go, then," Steve called over his shoulder as he ran down to the dock.

"How can I refuse? You're bigger than me." Paul donned a yellow rain slicker and threw a baseball cap over his patchy hair.

The downpour had lessened to a cool, steady rain. Steve didn't care if he got wet. Neither did Paul, who loved any chance to start up *Wild Lady*'s engines. He really enjoyed taking the long, sleek, deafeningly loud boat out for a spin.

"Where we going, boss?" Paul asked.

"Just take it slow along the shore for a bit."

"I thought you wanted a fast boat."

"I do. I may. Besides, your slow is always fast anyway."

"Is this a police matter?" Paul pushed forward on the throttle. "You doing this for Alec? Am I gonna be compensated? This machine of mine uses a lot of juice, boss." He patted the console of his boat.

"You'll be compensated," Steve said evenly. If he had to compensate Paul himself, he would.

As he scanned the horizon in the rain, he hoped he wasn't too late. *God,* he prayed, *she has to be okay.*

Two years ago when he had come back to God, it was with the realization that he couldn't keep his life together on his own. He thought he could. He'd trusted his own strength—and there was plenty of that. He had never looked for God before in his life because he hadn't needed God. He had gotten by with his own wiles, his size, his strength, his superb training, which had given him abilities far beyond most civilians.

But in two years he was learning that all of his strength was weakness when compared to God's.

Coming to know Nori had taken this whole journey one step further for him. He was beginning to trust another person, a woman. He was allowing himself to fall in love. And now he was about to lose Nori because of his own pride.

Fifteen minutes later, Steve saw something floating on the lake, far off in the distance.

"Over there," he said to Paul, pointing. "Quick."

Wild Lady roared over the top of the waves to the floating shape. From some distance away, he saw that it was an empty kayak.

It was Nori's kayak!

"Slow down. Put it in Neutral. Let me grab the kayak." He grabbed *Wild Lady*'s boat hook, and he leaned over and grabbed the line from the kayak's bow.

"Whose boat?" Paul asked.

"It might be the person who's in danger."

Paul frowned, pushed his thick eyebrows together. "Where's the paddle?"

"Good question." Was Nori wearing her PFD? Had she been pursued on the water, taken from her kayak?

The sky lit up behind him. Lightning was on its way.

"What to do, boss?" Paul asked. "Last time I was out in lightning, it blew out my whole electronics. Cost me a bundle to get it replaced. I was lucky she didn't blow a hole right through my boat."

Steve scanned the lake. He wasn't going back. He was going to find Nori. "I'll buy you a new boat," Steve said. "I have to find her."

"Okay then, where to, boss?"

"Let's go along the shoreline, like before. You look toward the shore on the right and I'll keep focused on the left shore. Look for anything out of the ordinary. We'll let the kayak drift. We can always get it later and it will slow us down." Steve threw the kayak's line away from *Wild Lady*.

An hour later they had covered the area from East Bay to Johnson's Bay and all around Twin Peaks Island. Now they were slowly heading back up the shore toward Trail's End.

Still no sign of Nori. Was he too late?

Even though the thought of going anywhere on her ankle made her cringe, Nori knew they needed to get away from here and they needed to leave soon. Joe would be back at any moment. When Chase said that Joe would kill him if he didn't carry out the plans, Nori knew he meant every word.

"You know you need to talk to the police. This

has to be resolved. And I think the police will find Joe the only one who's responsible," Nori said.

"But we helped," Selena said. "Joe said we were in as deep as he was, if not more."

Joe had really wrapped these kids around his little finger. "Let the police decide that. You know you need to get this off your chest, whatever the outcome. But I'm sure they'll be lenient."

"If we could only be lenient on ourselves," Selena added.

Once the two were convinced they needed to leave, the question of how to escape became the main issue. If they walked overland along the rough trail, Joe could easily find them. Their only chance was along the shore.

Nori said, "It's rough here. I know this area. There are places where there is no beach, and we'll be scrambling over rocks and branches and wading out into the water. But it's our only chance. We have to try."

Before they left, Chase put up his hand and said, "You guys wait here for a minute."

"We don't have much time."

"I'll be right back."

A few moments later he came back with a thick, strong piece of green wood. He said to Nori, "You can use it for a walking stick."

"Thank you, Chase."

"I tried to find one with a top that's sort of like a handle."

"That was very thoughtful of you." She tried it. Although it could have been two inches longer for her tall frame, it would work. It was certainly a lot better than hobbling and trusting her weight to whatever scrub brushes she could grab along the trail.

She figured it was about four or five miles to Trail's End, where they could get into her truck and make it to town.

After only about half a mile, the three of them were drenched. The rain was light, but steady. Her ankle was swollen and hurting. She was thankful for the stick, which was proving to be heavy enough to bear her weight. Her feet were sopping right through her running shoes and her jacket felt like a dirty, wet mop against her back.

The two beside her kept pace, helping her often. They talked little. All three of them were intent on putting as much distance between them and Joe as possible. Nori had an idea that Chase and Selena were reliving the horror of that night. In her soul, Nori felt their innocence. They had just gotten caught up in a horrible, horrible accident. Joe was the one who gone to the party with the gun. He was the one who had aimed it at Scott.

Everything had escalated from there and she knew Joe had kept the kids under his thumb with threats of blackmail.

Even if these kids were found innocent, however, they were a long way from being whole. It would take time and lots of counseling. But these kids were strong. They would come through it. Nori was certain of it. This was the first step.

Then there was Steve. She wondered if the two of them had a future. Probably not. She couldn't think about that now. She needed to get these kids to safety. That was her first concern. Then she would clean up the mess that was her life. She would put Trail's End up for sale and then go and try to make a home for herself and her daughters in some other place.

It was the unmistakable sounds of *Wild Lady* that made them stop and gaze out at the lake.

"It's Paul," Selena said. "In his cigarette boat."

They were some distance from the water and were hiking rather slowly through a rough patch of lakefront. To get down to where *Wild Lady* could even see them, they would have to make it over rocks and through grasses and swamp. But they had to try.

Chase had already made it to the shore and stood knee-deep in the black water. Nori followed, testing her walking stick in the mud.

Chase turned to her. "He could be way across the lake. Sounds travel farther over water."

"Wave anyway," Selena said.

Chase took off his jacket and waved wildly over his head.

But they were too far away. She could hear the sound of the engine receding in the distance.

TWENTY

Steve scanned the lake, oblivious to the distant thunder and the rain, which kept spotting his binoculars. He didn't care. He just wanted to find Nori. He needed to see her. He hoped it wouldn't be facedown inside of a PFD, floating on the top of the waves. He thought about the blood he had seen on the rocks in front of her lodge. He didn't know how all the pieces of the puzzle fit together, but one thing he did know was that she was not part of whatever had happened to Heather and Scott.

There was so much he needed to apologize for, doubting her—even for a second. As he searched the surface of the lake for her, worry in every cell of his body, he thought about the fact that all she wanted was a place to call home—*what we all want,* he thought. And now she was caught up in something that wasn't even about her.

Please God, he prayed, *help me find her. It can't be too late.*

"Paul, I want you to take this boat a bit closer to the shore."

Despite Steve's vigilance, it was Paul who saw someone waving on the shore.

"Boss?" he said.

Steve aimed his binoculars in that direction. "Head over there."

"Will do." Paul pushed forward on the throttle, and *Wild Lady* leaped in the direction of the shore.

As he got closer Steve saw three figures through the rain. Could it be . . . ? Yes, it was! Nori! Plus, surprisingly, Selena and Chase. What were they doing on that outcropping of rock? How did they get up there, and why?

"Nori!" he yelled, cupping his hands around his mouth. "Nori!"

"Steve!" Selena called, jumping up and down. "Over here."

But his eyes were not on Selena. Or Chase. He could see only Nori, drenched, standing very still, her hands at her sides, looking at him. He couldn't even guess what she was thinking.

"Nori! I'm here."

Maybe she was just exhausted, and she certainly looked tired, but to him she had never looked more beautiful. She was walking stiff-legged toward the edge of the rock. He couldn't read the expression on her face. She wasn't looking at him. Did she mean to climb down the rock face?

"Get back," he called to the three of them. "Don't try to climb down this rock. It's too slippery in the rain."

Selena had already descended the rock near the shore and Chase reached forward and grabbed Nori's arm to steer her back over and down the side toward a marshy beach.

Next to the rock was a marshy stretch of

lakeshore. But Steve didn't care how marshy it was, or how wet he was.

Steve threw off his jacket, pulled off his sandals and climbed over the side of *Wild Lady*. He was waist-deep among the lily pads and bulrushes. The sky was dark and the rain kept falling. He had eyes for only one person on the shore—Nori.

Nori, sandals off, was stepping carefully through stones, marsh weeds and sand. In moments he had reached her and, without thinking, without caring, he took her into his arms and held her close. There was a pinprick of a moment when he thought she might back away. But she didn't. She seemed to fall into his arms, and it took him a moment to realize that the heaving of her shoulders was not cold or shivering. She was crying. It grieved him that he could be the source.

"Nori. Oh, Nori." He stroked her back. "I'm sorry, Nori. I never should have doubted you. Will you ever forgive me?"

She backed away, just enough to look into his face, and said one word. "Yes."

It was all he needed.

"Boss?" Paul was calling from the boat. "We need to make tracks, boss."

"He's coming back!" Chase yelled.

"He has a gun!" Selena called.

Steve looked up in time to see Joe on a quad, motoring toward them down the slick path. Chase and Selena, shoulder-deep in marshy water, were being helped onto the boat by Paul. "Hurry, boss."

As quick as he could, Steve picked up Nori, held her in his arms and carried and swam with her to the waiting boat.

"Paul," he called. "If you have any blankets get them out."

"Will do, boss."

Suddenly two quick shots rang out, and water spouted from two places about thirty feet from shore.

"Go, go, go," he yelled to Paul.

"But where are you going?" Nori called frantically when Steve pushed the boat away with his forearm.

"I have to take care of a certain something," he said before plunging down into the marshy water.

Holding his breath and swimming with all his might, Steve made it to a stand of tall reeds and ducked down behind.

Only his eyes and ears were out of the water when he heard three more shots. Joe had jumped off his quad and was running the last hundred yards toward the shore, firing his pistol at the retreating boat.

Steve heard another shot and a loud click.

Joe's pistol was empty, and Steve now knew who was going to be in control. Ten years of Special Ops experience was more than a match for a scared and angry twenty-year-old. Joe was standing in the lake now, gazing at the retreating boat.

The look on Joe's face was utter terror when Steve burst from the water, weeds hanging from his head and water streaming from his hair. Two huge hands grabbed Joe's jacket.

When Paul returned ten minutes later, Steve forced Joe into the boat, his hands tied behind his back with his own shoelaces. The empty gun was stuck in Steve's belt.

"Watched it all with the binoculars," Paul said. "You looked like an action hero coming out of the water at Joe."

"I guess he wasn't expecting the creature from the deep coming up at him like that," said Steve.

Nori, Selena and Chase were wrapped in blankets from the supplies up in the front of the boat. Towels, blankets and dry clothes were always in their waterproof plastic containers. Paul kept a safe boat. With the three hostages freed, dried and warm, they decided to pick up the kayak rather than screaming home at fifty miles per hour. The prisoner, Joe, was talking a blue streak about how it was all an accident, how he really didn't mean to hurt anybody and how he was so much in love with Heather.

"Save it for the sheriff, Joe," growled Steve.

Steve kept his arm around Nori, and he liked the

way she nestled into him. Maybe there was a chance for them. Just before they reached the town wharf, she looked up at him, rain glistening on her lashes, and said, "Do you know, Mr. Baylor, this is the second time you've rescued me in the rain?"

EPILOGUE

The next two weeks had been crazy and strange. Nori had stayed at Bette's until the investigation at Trail's End had been completed. They found the remains of Heather Malloy and Scott Gramble near Cabin 10 where Joe had buried them.

Joe had told the police that when Heather had dropped him, his world had collapsed. He had come to the party with the gun because he wanted to threaten Scott, show him who was boss. His plan was to get Scott alone in the woods and scare him off.

His plans took a tragic turn when Heather showed up as Joe was aiming the gun at Scott. But once all the craziness started, he tried to coerce the kids into taking the blame. It had almost worked, too.

Nori had been right. The judge had been lenient with Chase, Selena, Blaine, Meredith, Connolly and the other kids who'd been at Trail's End during the time of the deaths. All of them had to undergo counseling plus perform community service. Chase seemed to be enjoying his role as a mural painter's assistant.

A week after the investigation, Nori had moved back to Trail's End.

All through the early months of summer, Nori and Steve spent a lot of time talking. They decided to take it slowly. Both of them needed time. Nori had loved only one man in her whole life. Was there space in her heart for another? And Steve had been hurt—his neglect of his family had driven them away. Could he trust himself that this wouldn't happen with Nori?

They talked and talked. They started attending a home Bible study, where they learned that God had to be first in their lives. When you put God first, everything else fell into place.

All these thoughts swirled through Nori's head as she stood putting the finishing touches on the building mural.

It was the end of the summer now and Nori was just about finished with the mural. She climbed down from the scaffolding, crossed the street and leaned against a storefront to get a view of the entire painting. Daphne and Rachel would love it—she knew they would.

"Well, Marty, I've finished the mural and it's time to say goodbye. I've found someone I know you would approve of. You know I will always love you, but God has shown me this is where I should be and that Steve is who I am to be with."

"Were you talking to me, Nori?" called Chase.

"No, sorry—just thinking out loud. So what do you think, Chase? You think this adds to Marlene's Café?"

The young man nodded and grinned. Throughout the summer months Chase had proved to be a valuable worker—good with color, good with detail and even a good researcher. Painting a mural was not like working on a canvas, even a very large canvas. A mural on the side of a building required many gallons of paint. She would outline the drawings and Chase would fill them in with great rollers of paint. She'd been working on it for almost two months and it was just about finished. Her goal was to get it done today. Today her daughters were finally coming to Trail's End, and she wanted everything to be perfect.

As the painting of the mural had progressed, Marlene continually said she loved the scene with the old lake schooner coming down between Twin Peaks Island and Moose Island under full sail, the sun turning the canvas sails golden.

Marlene said the whole thing would be good for tourism. Whisper Lake boasted more than just ghosts. Old Captain Winston Abercrombie, who'd retired here after the Loyalists had left, had built just such a boat and sailed it on this lake until he died. It was what Marlene wanted. The place would now be called The Schooner Café.

"I'll just go and finish the bottom edge," Chase said. "But I still think the old Union Jack isn't quite right. Let me work on it."

Nori grinned. "You are becoming such a perfectionist, Chase. It's fine, it really is. Just go finish the bottom edge."

She unscrewed the top of her thermos. Not too bad, she thought. Not too bad at all.

"I like it," she said to no one in particular.

"So do I."

Nori turned. Steve was there. And smiling broadly.

"Don't get too close." She laughed. "I'm covered in paint."

"That's never stopped me before," he said, taking her into a close embrace. He backed away only far enough so they could talk. "I've been thinking about church, Nori."

"I guess I'm becoming a regular there." She smiled up at him.

"Well, I think we need to talk with the pastor." Steve's grin widened.

"About what?"

Steve let go of her then and got down on one knee right there on the sidewalk. "We need to talk to the pastor if we are going to have him marry us."

And with that, the most beautiful diamond ring Nori had ever seen appeared in the palm of Steve's big hand.

Dear Reader,

Do you long for "home"? Do you yearn for that place where you fit perfectly and where you can be totally yourself and it's okay? All of us desire that, I think. Even when we are in our own houses, sometimes the feeling of *home* eludes us. It did for Nori. Ever since her husband died she'd been searching for home. She wasn't finding it. Even packing up and moving to an entirely new place just didn't do it for her. She complained to Steve that she couldn't turn Trail's End into home no matter how hard she tried.

Eventually she finds that place. But it takes her a long time.

Storm Warning is the first book in my new Whisper Lake series. It's quite fun to happily explore the life and loves of the people who inhabit the small town of Whisper Lake Crossing, Maine. Whisper Lake is a fictional place, but it's not unlike many small lake towns in Maine that I've been fortunate enough to spend time in.

I also love stories within stories, and in *Storm Warning*, not only do you have the story of how Nori and Steve meet and fall in love, but you also get the story of Molly and James, the people who built Trail's End to be their home. It worked for a while for them—but only for a while. Their stories interweave throughout the book.

I don't believe that any of us truly come home until we find our "home" in God. In Psalm 90:1, God promises to be more than our God. He promises to be our dwelling place. Stop and think about that for a moment. This is saying that none of us are ever really home until He takes up residence within us.

If you have any comments of your own about "home," or about anything I have written, I love hearing from you, and I promise to answer. I can be reached at:
Linda@writerhall.com. I also invite you to my Web site, www.writerhall.com.

Linda Hall

QUESTIONS FOR DISCUSSION

1. All Nori wants to do is provide a home for herself and her daughters, a place that feels good and a place that fits them. That's why she buys Trail's End. Describe what "being home" means to you.

2. Not only does Nori want a home, but she wants to start over. Have you ever come to a place in your life when you wanted to begin all over again? Describe the circumstances. Was this something you actually did?

3. Nori is sure that Molly's life resembles her own. Do you agree with her assessment? Or is Nori seeing coincidences that aren't there? Why or why not?

4. A few times in the story, Nori becomes convinced that Trail's End is inhabited by the ghost of Molly Jones. Would you have come to the same conclusion?

5. Do you think the name Trail's End fits the place that Nori bought? Why or why not? Describe your perfect Trail's End.

6. *Storm Warning* begins with a storm on the lake, and storms or the threat of storms figure into the book. Yet in the end Nori and Steve discover that God is the great storm calmer. Is there a storm in your life right now that needs calming? Why not give that storm to God?

7. Steve blames himself for the breakup of his marriage and doesn't think God will forgive him. And more important, he doesn't think he's worthy of any woman's love. Is there something in your life that you don't think God can forgive?

8. Throughout the story Steve grows into a person who can trust again. How does he gradually become a person that Nori can love? Do you think the two of them are a good fit? Why?

9. Nori's friend Lisa arrives just at the right time. Has God ever brought a friend into your life just at the right time? Describe.

10. The teens in Whisper Lake Crossing are keeping a deadly secret, a secret that almost destroys them. Have you ever held on to a deadly secret? What should they have done from the beginning? Would you have done what they did? Why or why not?

11. After Nori's husband dies, she found it difficult to paint again. Have you ever found it difficult to return to some task that you formerly loved? What were the circumstances? What got you past it?

12. Psalm 90:1 says that God is not only our God but our dwelling place—in other words, our home. Is God your dwelling place? How can you make Him so?

LINDA HALL

When people ask award-winning author Linda Hall when it was that she got the "bug" for writing, she answers that she was probably born with a pencil in her hand. Linda has always loved reading and would read far into the night, way past when she was supposed to turn her lights out. She still enjoys reading and probably reads a novel a week.

She also loved to write, and drove her childhood friends crazy wanting to spend summer afternoons making up group stories. She's carried that love into adulthood with twelve novels.

Linda has been married for thirty-five years to a wonderful and supportive husband who reads everything she writes and who is always her first editor. The Halls have two children and three grandchildren.

Growing up in New Jersey, her love of the ocean was nurtured during many trips to the shore. When she's not writing, she and her husband enjoy sailing the St. John River system and the coast of Maine in their twenty-eight-foot sailboat, *Gypsy Rover II.*

Linda loves to hear from her readers and can be contacted at Linda@writerhall.com. She invites her readers to her Web site which includes her blog and pictures of her sailboat: http://writerhall.com.

Center Point Publishing
600 Brooks Road ● PO Box 1
Thorndike ME 04986-0001 USA

(207) 568-3717

US & Canada:
1 800 929-9108
www.centerpointlargeprint.com